# Out of That World

# Out of That World

Jill Staynes

**FABER & FABER**
London · Boston

First published in 1979
by Faber and Faber Limited
3 Queen Square London WC1N 3AU
Printed in Great Britain by
The Bowering Press Ltd Plymouth

© Jill Staynes 1979

British Library Cataloguing in Publication Data

Staynes, Jill
  Out of that world.
  I. Title
  823'.9'1J      PZ7.S/

  ISBN 0-571-11302-8

# CHAPTER
 1

Bertie hadn't expected to like Longbarrow, and was quite satisfied to find it was every bit as gloomy as she had imagined. As she paid the taxi she thought the whole house could do with a good wash, windows included. Even the ivy looked dusty as it peered limply in.

The taxi-man, large and disagreeable in a greasy jacket, was not going to help her in with her cases. He turned his back on them as they stood in a forlorn twosome on the gravel, and climbed back into the taxi. Bertie was sure he despised the tip she'd given him. It was stupid to be put out when people you weren't ever going to see again didn't think much of you, but it was always happening.

As the taxi scrunched away between the rhododendrons she faced the house and picked up a case in either hand. Her arms seemed to lengthen in their sockets like a gorilla's. The door opened as she was coming up the steps in a kind of crouching run, and a woman stood there, gloomed by the porch.

"Oh, dear, we weren't expecting you today. Your uncle said it was tomorrow you were coming. What a pity!"

Bertie felt about as wanted as the plague. She said nothing, however, as there didn't seem to be anything suitable to say, and was at least relieved of her cases, which the woman seemed tough enough to manage. The hall was darker than the porch, and full of plants, most of which appeared to have given up the struggle, for which Bertie did not blame them.

"This way, dear. You had better go straight to your room, as your uncle won't want to see you yet."

Charming, thought Bertie as she followed the woman up a twisting, sloping staircase. Pity I can't let him know how little I want to see him. She slipped on one of the steps turning the corner, and the woman called over her shoulder:

"Mind out, dear. These stairs are very treacherous."

They wouldn't be quite so treacherous, Bertie considered, if they had not been gone over, probably by the woman herself—who must be the housekeeper—with a polish designed to bring one to one's knees. Useful in a monastery, perhaps.

Her room smelt of polish but it was surprisingly nice, even though a bit like something out of the Victoria and Albert Museum. Bertie couldn't help feeling cheered by the four-poster, in spite of the dark red, dusty-looking curtains, and a suspicion that there were spiders taking their ease on the tester who might later clamber down to inspect the occupant. She definitely looked forward to telling Mother about the four-poster.

The woman was chatting on, now she had dumped the cases. Bertie decided that she looked like an elderly horse. The face was kindly, but not backed by any blinding intelligence. There were several chins which wobbled enthusiastically as she spoke and made it rather difficult to attend to what she was saying. Climbing the stairs with suitcases had made her out of breath and loosened the hairpins with which she kept up her knot of abundant white hair so that they stuck out in a frantic fan.

"Such a nuisance we didn't know you were coming today, dear, or you could have been met at the station. I daresay your uncle would have sent for Moss to pick you up in the car, you know, though he doesn't think he's safe in it, really, but then it's so old I don't know who is. I hope you don't mind bread and cheese and soup for lunch, dear, I haven't anything else in the house and your uncle won't let me open a tin."

She was busy fiddling with the catches on the suitcases in a remarkably clumsy way and Bertie wondered if her uncle's ruling was intended to prevent gore in the tomato soup. The catch on the suitcase suddenly flew open, striking the housekeeper sharply on the knuckles. Hairpins showered the carpet.

Bertie went down on her knees to pick them up, and suddenly for no reason she could think of found herself wondering how Daddy was. She was still sure she could have been of some use helping Mother to look after him, instead of scrambling about after this idiot woman's hairpins, miles away, in a place she didn't want to be.

"I'll have to break it to your uncle that you're here, before lunch, thank you, dear, I think that's the lot but I couldn't bear to have it cut, or he won't like being surprised by the sight of you. Not that I wouldn't know you anywhere for what you are, you've a great look of Mr. Featherstone's sister, your grandmother I suppose, really, even though I do call him your uncle, great-uncle is too much of a mouthful, isn't it? And speaking of mouthfuls, I'd better go and heat up the soup or I'll be late with the lunch, and that would never do."

She was hurrying out of the room, sticking pins in her hair, when she stopped to look back anxiously.

"Come down when you've tidied, dear, won't you, I should unpack afterwards or you might be late and you don't want to make a bad impression on your uncle when he's so particular. Down the stairs, turn left, and that's the dining-room. I must fly."

She bustled from the room and Bertie heard her shoes squeaking on those awful stairs.

Bertie was glad the old thing—what was her name, Mother had told her, Squidgy or something—hadn't stayed after all to help her unpack, she didn't want strangers looking at her under-clothes and anyway, she had had to pack in a hurry and every-thing was in a mess. Mother wouldn't have approved of her slip-pers rolled in her nightie, either, though Bertie would have quite liked old Squidgy to see those new bras she had got, with orange tulips on, and the green and gold frock she had bought to go to Italy. She suddenly slammed the lid down again on her huddled clothes, and looked out of the window with eyes that rainbowed the gravel and made the ivy swim. It should have been Florence, not Longbarrow; sunshine, not an English summer. How could you ever trust Providence again, if it let you down like this? She

3

was still busy not believing what had happened; suppose it slipped in a further blow before she'd got used to the ones she had?

Somewhere a clock struck a hollow note. Another, in the depths of the house, groaned, summoned up all its energy and followed the example. Lunch, thought Bertie, galvanised, and rushed to the dressing-table to look at her reflection in the mirror. A quick brush of the hair; the brush was at the bottom of the suitcase and in dragging it out she spilt half the clothes on the floor and left them there, no time to find the bathroom to wash her hands, and Great-Uncle will have to lump the first impression. If he's so particular he won't like me anyway, she told her face grinning with agony under a tangle.

Of course, the stairs were lying in wait for her, and she skidded on the bend, but, apart from getting her hands even greasier by braking on the walls—that woman polished everything, lucky the ceilings weren't panelled—she managed without actually sitting down. The dining-room was on the left, too, and in her relief at finding it she charged in without thinking about anything except that she was amazingly hungry and ready for any amount of bread and cheese.

The room was large and dark, the chief feature a huge polished (of course) table with pewter candlesticks standing mournfully down its length, and a window at the far end. A man was standing with his back to it, his hands on a tall chair facing her. She couldn't see his face because the light was behind him, but there was something so essentially forbidding about his height, and his silence that she didn't need to be told this was Great-Uncle Felix. She wished she hadn't come into the room like a tornado with an appetite.

"Ah, Roberta." He had a dry, disapproving voice, like that of a schoolmaster commenting on an unsatisfactory end-of-term report: "Mrs. Pigeon has just told me about you. A pity you didn't arrive when you were expected."

"Mother wrote to you, I thought."

"Your mother has never had a very acute sense of time, and none at all of history. I hope you are interested in history? If we are to have any civilised conversation, you will have to cultivate a feeling for the fourth dimension."

Mother said he was odd, but she never told me he was clean off his trolley, and even the trolley nowhere in sight. Bertie muttered something in what Daddy called her sotto voice but Great-Uncle Felix wasn't easily fobbed off. He leant forward over the chair and said sharply,

"What's that? Clarity is the first essential of communication. Speak up. I'm not deaf and I won't have anyone pretending I am."

Luckily for Bertie, who was clearing her throat to get out something desperate about liking history at school, the door behind her opened and Mrs. Pigeon came in with a tray and three bowls of soup. Great-Uncle Felix was so busy peering at his bowl that he forgot to follow up his unpromising conversational opening.

"What's this, Mrs. Pigeon? Carrot soup? I hope you used the carrots Moss gathered. He swears he has employed no chemical fertiliser at all, but I don't know how far you can trust a man with a television set."

Stark bats, thought Bertie, following the example of her great-uncle and Mrs. Pigeon, who was busy protesting she had indeed used the Moss carrots, in sitting down and taking up a spoon. The only thing I can't understand is why he hasn't got shut up. A fantasy in which she supposed that perhaps he had, and she was really visiting a private lunatic asylum, with Mrs. Pigeon as keeper, entertained her as she drank the carrot soup, an alarming orange but not bad at all.

"I suppose there's no better news of your father? Why people want to go rushing about in cars I haven't the least idea. I only keep one because there's no one here any more who knows how to look after a horse. If these ridiculous machines get more of a hold on people than they've got already we'll all be living in caravans and the countryside'll be nothing but motorways in between the towns."

"Oh, Mr. Featherstone, what a horrible idea, you mustn't suggest it. How is your father, dear, I did mean to ask when I saw you but things do go out of my head so."

Bertie wished things didn't come back into her head, because if there was one thing she didn't want to talk about, it was her father. She didn't even want to think about him.

"The doctors say he's as well as can be expected." The phrase she always hated to hear herself seemed quite useful to offer them now.

"Your poor mother. It all must have been a terrible shock to her. What a pity you couldn't have kept her company and cheered her up a little. It will be a great comfort, though, her having your grandmother to stay with."

"I doubt it." Great-Uncle Felix was champing a crust of bread scraped over with margarine, and his grey moustache performed some very complicated movements which Bertie had to watch. "My sister's about as much comfort as a sick hen. Eating all that denaturised food's taken all the energy out of her."

Bertie remembered her grandmother as quite energetic enough when it came to criticising her, but it was clear Great-Uncle Felix had unusual standards of judgement. Bertie tried also to recollect the sort of food she had eaten in her grandmother's house. Her memories of meals there were somewhat clouded by being conscious that her table manners were under observation, and that always turned food to sawdust. What was 'denaturised'?

Mrs. Pigeon had taken away the soup bowls and was bringing in the next course. It seemed to be a sort of cheese salad, lots of lettuce—and it was nice and crisp and not the sort of exhausted stuff you got escorting sandwiches—and large chunks of cheddar cheese, tomato and apple. There was green pepper, too, chopped up and very crunchy. Great-Uncle Felix masticated with relish, his moustache working overtime.

"Won't get anything better than this, you know. Pure vitamin C. You get more of it in green pepper than in anything else. We always have a green pepper every day. Got to be raw, though, you destroy half its value if you cook it."

Mrs. Pigeon's face, Bertie thought, wore a faintly resigned expression, as though providing a green pepper every day and refraining from cooking it was not the least of her burdens. Bertie chumped her lettuce and pepper, the noise she made in her own ears only equalled by the robust barrage put up by Great-Uncle Felix, and, to a lesser and more demure degree, by Mrs. Pigeon. We must look like a family of rabbits, she thought, and silently crowned Mrs. Pigeon with a poke-bonnet resembling that of

6

Jemima Puddle-duck, and her great uncle with Benjamin Bunny's tam-o-shanter. It was under this invisible and rakish headgear that he turned to address her.

"And what do you intend to do while you're with us? Study, take long walks, write a book?"

Bertie was rather stunned. Studying was not something she was keen on in the holidays, though of course it was true she was supposed to be getting on with reading *A Tale of Two Cities*, which was the set novel for next June's O Level, but that was a year away and no one could be expected to be serious about it yet. Long walks—that wasn't her style at all. Long strolls, perhaps, if she happened to be walking and thinking about something else at the same time. As for writing a book, he must be joking? People her age didn't write books, but probably he was so far detached from his trolley that this hadn't sunk in.

"I wasn't really meaning to do anything in particular."

"Great mistake." Her great-uncle had pounced with some satisfaction; Bertie got the impression that this was the reply he had been hoping for. "Great mistake not to have an Aim. If you don't have an Aim you'll never achieve anything."

"She's only fifteen, Mr. Featherstone, after all."

"That makes no difference. If you don't start setting yourself aims when you're fifteen you end up at fifty without anything to show for the years in between."

"Except perhaps a husband." Mrs. Pigeon looked almost coy. Great-Uncle Felix stared, and his moustache jumped scornfully.

"Absurd. What has a husband got to do with it? Any girl can marry if she takes the trouble. Doesn't take any intelligence to fall in love and all that sort of rubbish. Dare say you did it."

Mrs. Pigeon did not take this as the insult it had sounded to Bertie, but smiled almost dreamily, and nodded. Bertie was suddenly sorry for her. Presumably her husband was dead, or she wouldn't be housekeeping for Great-Uncle Felix, and, to judge by her expression, she must have loved her husband. Bertie turned her attention fiercely to the bread and cheese which had succeeded the salad. Evidently cheese was a favourite thing in this household.

"You thinking of marrying?"

7

Bertie swallowed some cheese in a hurry. "Well, not yet." Didn't he have any idea of how old she was? He must have, because Mrs. Pigeon had mentioned it, and was doing so again.

"She's only fifteen, Mr. Featherstone."

"You keep saying that. I'm not deaf, you know. Some girls think of marrying someone or other from the moment they give up dolls. Most girls of her age are permanently in love. It's a sort of yeast," Great-Uncle Felix smacked his lips over the word, "a yeast in the blood."

Bertie was furious to find herself blushing. Of course she was in love with several people, quite a few of them dead, like Cesare Borgia and Alexander the Great, and some alive, like Nureyev, though she didn't feel anything special about the boys she knew; but people had no right to talk about such things openly, it was like mental undressing. She felt her face go hot down to her chest, and saw, wthout looking up, that Mrs. Pigeon had tactfully started to stare out of the window, but nothing was going to stop Great-Uncle Felix.

"All you can do is to live through it, it's a disease only time can cure. Try not to marry while you've got it, that's all, or you'll end up in the divorce courts."

Bertie amazed herself by throwing down her knife and bursting into tears. Through a sparkling haze she saw, like a kaleidoscope, fragments of Mrs. Pigeon's startled face, her uncle's mouth half open under the momentarily frozen moustache; and then, without her arranging it in any way, she found her body had carried her out of the room at much the same rush with which she had entered it.

As she ran upstairs to her room she heard the ominous thunder of the dining-room door as it slammed shut after her.

# CHAPTER

2

It was quite a relief, crying at last, especially as she hadn't really given way, she just couldn't help it. It was as though all her feelings of misery and incredulity, her terror over the possibility of Daddy and Mother breaking up, her terror over the car crash that had given Daddy another chance with Mother, even all the wretched little pinpricks, like the taxi-driver's expression when he looked down at the money in his dirty hand, and Mrs. Pigeon's dismay when she opened the door, had been piling up like matter in a boil, and now it had burst. What a disgusting idea, thought Bertie, remembering a frightful time when she had had two boils, and how sympathetic it had made her feel towards Job—but it's just right for what has happened. She felt cleaner in her mind for crying, and it was with some satisfaction that she measured off a finger's length against the damp patch she had made on the red coverlet. It smelt dusty round the patch, and the patch itself smelt of mildew.

A door opened and shut downstairs and Bertie sat up in a hurry. Was someone going to come up after her and start scolding her or wanting explanations or something awful? She listened intently, pulling back the hair from her ears. Footsteps crossed the hall, another door opened and shut somewhere. Perhaps that was her great-uncle going to his study. She didn't think he would have come up, anyway, it was Mrs. Pigeon blundering in among her feelings she was afraid of. So she meant well and she seemed a nice old thing but it was none of her business. The door opened again and the unmistakable shoes creaked in the hall; they stopped—at the foot of the stairs? Bertie held her breath. They creaked on, and there was the sound of a door pushed open and swinging to, with a settling boom, a door designed for people with trays, and doubtless leading to the kitchen.

Bertie began to breathe more normally, but her chief thought was still how to avoid questioning, or sympathy. Probably she ought to go and say she was sorry for rushing out rudely like that, but seeing anybody would be impossible. She had to get out of this house for a bit, and think about all of it.

She pulled a paper hanky out of her bag, wetted it from her witch-hazel bottle and held it to her eyes for a minute until they felt cooler. Then she put her hair further over her face and went to the door. Could she get down those ghastly glass stairs without Mrs. Pigeon in the kitchen or Great-Uncle Felix in his study hearing her?

She did, however, and tiptoed across to the hall door. No doubt there was a door at the back, easier to get out of, but as she didn't know where it was she was safer to risk making a slight noise with this one. She nearly fell over the clutter of plants in the entry, then delicately, carefully, turned the knob and stepped out. She shut the door behind her like a burglar, and tiptoed across the stone terrace that went round the house, to the left as the study seemed to be to the right, and the kitchen at the back. Mother had said there was a large garden—it was one of the things she had tried to comfort her with—and there must be a place in it where people wouldn't find her immediately and she could take time to feel better.

The terrace led round the side of the house; it had little turreted bits with flat stones on at the corner. She would have sat on one, it looked so inviting and just bottom-height, only she was afraid someone might look out of a window or come out of a door before she had time to get into the safety of the garden. As she turned the corner of the house, she saw the terrace ran along the back wall also, with some shallow steps in the middle and a brick path to an opening in a tall hedge opposite. The windows of the kitchen might overlook the terrace at the far end, however, and she impulsively swung a leg over the low wall on to the grass and ran quickly to the hedge-opening, avoiding the terrace altogether. Only as she dashed through the opening did it occur to her that it would have been easier to escape observation if she had hugged the wall of the house, as no one would have seen her unless actually leaning out of a window. Super Robin Hood I'd have made. No wonder his men were merry, probably splitting themselves to their Lincoln green drawers watching their leader catching his feet in the ferns.

The prickling sensation on the back of her neck calmed down as she hurried into what seemed the denser part of the garden, along a path bordered on one side by roses growing thickly on a support of rustic branches like arbours without tops. On the other side was another, very tall, dark green hedge that looked nice and protective. Perhaps she could get behind it? There was an opening, further on, narrow and dark with shadow. In it she stopped to appreciate what she saw.

The great hedge, perhaps seven foot tall, certainly more than a man's height, ran all the way round an enclosure of lawn that seemed as big as a bowling green and as smooth. With just the sky above and the afternoon sunlight on the grass, it looked as private and peaceful a place as one could wish. Bertie breathed in the smell of the hedge, the scent of the roses in the walk behind her and the hot lawn smell of the great outdoor room in front of her. It looked as though it needed dancing in, but not *any* kind of dance. Perhaps minuets, stately rows of people advancing and retreating, from sunshine to shadow, turning slowly to face one hedge wall after another.

The awful thing about imagination was that you weren't sure you couldn't make things happen just by picturing them. She hadn't seen people dancing or anything like that, but she'd had a horribly strong feeling that they might be doing it and she just couldn't see it. Though why that should be frightening Bertie didn't understand. Surely there was nothing frightening about people dancing?

She deliberately pinched the skin on her wrist, partly to prove she wasn't part of a dream that could run away with her, and partly to punish herself for getting worked up in broad daylight.

As broad as it comes, she said airily to herself, and stepped out of the darkness of the hedge on to the huge open lawn.

She wandered about for a bit, scuffing with her toes at little bits of grass—seen close to, the lawn wasn't quite so perfect, they'd had trouble with moles, she told herself knowledgeably—but before long she stopped pretending that somehow she didn't feel crowded—in all that space!—and made for the other hedge exit.

She found herself in another walk, with the lawn hedge on one side and on the other a slender railing, shoulder high, and beyond the railing an expanse of rough grass and meadow, leading in the distance to woods. This, then, was the edge of the garden, and it was rather a shock, as though civilisation had stopped at that point and left the country to get on by itself.

There was something very inviting, however, at the far end of the walk, on the corner, as it were, of the garden. A willow tree had been encouraged to make a great hoop of leaves right over the walk from hedge to railing, a dense hiding-place where she could dimly see, in the flickers of sunlight through the shifting branches, a white seat there.

It was like being drowned in the willow's hair, sitting there invisible and looking out through the leaves at the field beyond. Great-Uncle Felix certainly had some sound ideas on what ought to be in a garden. Bertie began to relax a little, put her head back against the wooden slats of the bench and looked up through the green at the blue coming and going above.

Perhaps everything was going to be all right, and she would be able to stick it here—if she could get away often enough to the garden, anyway. Maybe she could even go exploring in the woods, that is, if they belonged to Great-Uncle Felix and the old nutter said she could. Mother would die when she told her the kind of things he said.

Abruptly she sat up. While she was in the garden, at this very minute, while she was looking at the view through the willow, something ghastly might be happening, Mother, Daddy—Wildly, she beat her mind away from the holes it tried to dive into, making like a terrified animal for one dark idea after another, Mother crying and writing her a letter—which might be in the post now—Daddy dying, perhaps this very second. If she thought of it, it might happen.

She got up, and fell out of her sandal as she rushed away. She limped back and rehooked her big toe round the thong. As she bent down and gave a savage pull at the heel to give her foot a proper purchase on the sole, something seemed to hit her on the ankle. She looked quickly to see if an insect had bitten her, but there was no mark. There was, however, a thing that glittered on the gravel. Could someone possibly have thrown it at her? That was what it had felt like, but there was no one about to throw it.

She picked up the glittering object and straightened herself with a head that swam suddenly. Stooping in the heat? She must be getting middle-aged at fifteen. All the same, she remembered Martine at school telling her earnestly that tons of your blood rushed to the head—or was it the feet?—when you stood up. Of course, Martine was so fat, poor thing, that one vaguely felt she must have more blood to do just that, only it must be just flesh she had more of, she was sure human beings were supposed to have almost the same amount of blood each.

However much she had, she was definitely feeling peculiar. She looked away from the thing in her hand—some kind of chipped stone with glassy edges that shone—to check on this. The distant woods seemed to waver, and the field between them run up to meet them. Bertie shut her eyes quickly.

When she opened them again everything seemed all right. She looked round cautiously, but the garden had stopped shimmering and the woods were behaving themselves. She must have stood up too quickly. Poor Martine, if that was what happened to her. No wonder she didn't exactly bound about.

The stone was rather a nice one, satisfying to hold. The fingers slipped easily over its facets; it would look good, too, beside her collection of stones from the seaside, at home. It was wedge-shaped, as though it had been sharpened to a point like a pencil. She put it into the big patch pocket on her skirt. Thank goodness she had some clothes with pockets, manufacturers were so mean about giving you an extra bit of material to keep things in. The only reason she had a pocket on this skirt was because Mother had made it. She had a sudden clear picture of Mother bending

13

over the stuff on the table at home, cutting it out, her scissors making that funny clacking noise on the wood underneath. Daddy didn't like the noise, though he didn't dislike it as much as the noise of knitting-needles. Mother had quite given up knitting now, and she had told Bertie she had done a lot of it at one time, before she had met Daddy. Daddy really was too difficult to live with, Bertie knew how much Mother felt that at times.

Bertie started to run along the path, away from the willow, and towards the house. If she met someone, she would have to talk, she wouldn't have to go on thinking about Daddy and Mother and what would happen if this last chance failed, and they decided to break up after all. She didn't stop to analyse the idea of talking to someone because she didn't want to imagine talking to either Mrs. Pigeon or Great-Uncle Felix, and there wasn't anyone else. Instead, she gave herself up to the physical sensation of pounding along the gravel, the smack of her feet in the cork soles, and the swing of her hair muffling her face or flying off it. She had satisfactorily stopped thinking when her sandal came off again.

When she had adjusted it, gripping the thong savagely between big and second toe, she realised she had reached one of the entrances to what she now thought of as the 'secret lawn', the great hedge-shut circle. She was about to go on—she might be looking for company but not the sort of company that lawn seemed, rather eerily, to have already—when she checked.

Someone was just moving out of the entrance opposite, into the walk on the other side.

It would have to be Great-Uncle Felix, because, from the glimpse she had caught, the figure was that of a man, and a tall one. Of course, it could be the gardener. Somebody had to keep that lawn cut that way, level as a dancing-floor, and those cliffs of hedges trimmed. If Great-Uncle Felix spent most of his time in the study, he wasn't the somebody, and, anyhow, he looked too frail an old nutter to cope.

Bertie hurried down the walk. Talking to a gardener would be much more fun than talking to Great-Uncle Felix; the gardener would hardly talk about Daddy and Mother, for a start.

There was no one in the other walk, no one in the little garden

14

with a rockery that it led to. Perhaps the gardener was one of the vanishing race of servants—Bertie thought this rather witty—who were trained to make themselves scarce if anyone turned up while they were working. Miss Mallors had said housemaids were supposed to fade into the wainscoting if they were caught dusting or anything incriminating like that. But surely gardening was O.K? P. G. Wodehouse let Lord Emsworth catch McPhee at his job, and he should know what went on.

No longer hurrying, in fact, scuffling the gravel slowly,—that thong was punishing her for gripping it so tightly—Bertie trailed back to the house. Her stomach told her it was time for something, probably tea. It seemed ages since she had burst out of lunch, crying, and left all that good bread and cheese on her plate.

It was going to be embarrassing, meeting them at tea after that. Bertie scowled, and hung her head so that her hair nearly met before her eyes. Mother would be shocked at her going in to tea with hands grubby from the garden but at the moment she felt a certain pleasure in being dirty and difficult. Great-Uncle Felix should jolly well see what sort of a person he had staying with him.

# CHAPTER

## 3

"To perform our role in life successfully, we need energy. Where do we get energy?"

Bertie chewed some rather gritty bread and hoped the question was rhetorical. Having tea on the terrace was not her idea of fun because she hated insects in her food, and was terrified of wasps, who always seemed to know if anyone was having tea out of doors. Telegraph service, that was it, little messenger wasps, brightly striped and saluting. Tea at Longbarrow, sir, terrace, west side. And the others, zooming out in formation. Check your stings, men. There'll be trouble.

"Energy, Roberta, comes from the food we eat. You cannot expect to run a car well on inferior fuel, or, indeed, if you forget to put in any petrol at all and make do with some other mixture the car cannot deal with. Have some of this on your bread. It is excellent."

It was dark brown and looked like the glue Daddy used to cook up on the stove when Mother wasn't in the kitchen. Bertie took some out of politeness. If it was honey, she had always liked the pale sort best.

"Molasses, Roberta, molasses. Learn the name so you can ask for it when you go home. The whole family would benefit if only you put them on the right path. I sincerely hope your father is being properly fed at this time. If he is to get well it is essential he should have concentrated energy foods of the highest quality."

Great-Uncle Felix masticated his bread indignantly, moustache moving in rhumba rhythm. "It is, of course, most unlikely Arabella is giving him anything of the kind. When I last had the misfortune to be entertained under her roof I was given white sugar and broiler chicken!"

Great-Uncle Felix stared round triumphantly, from Mrs. Pigeon to Bertie. Surely not both together, Bertie thought, with an hysterical picture of Great-Uncle Felix's moustache poised with horror over a mound of sugared chicken presented by her grandmother. Followed by deep-fried ice-cream, no doubt.

"What will you have to drink, dear?" Mrs. Pigeon didn't look happy, criticism of other people's housekeeping might be uncomfortably near criticism of one's own. "There's lemon-juice and brown sugar, or milk, if you like it better."

"Can I have tea, please, it's what I usually have." Bertie had asked before she realised there wasn't a teapot in front of Mrs. Pigeon. Great-Uncle Felix put down his tumbler, waving away a wasp with the back of his hand, and let loose.

"Tea! Do I understand your mother lets you have tea?"

"Yes, I've always had tea." Honestly, you'd think it was alcohol, the way he's looking. The wasp, disgustingly, had got stuck in her molasses.

"I shall never be able to understand the workings of the female mind. Mrs. Pigeon, here, drank tea all the time until she came to live at Longbarrow. Cup after cup. Poisoning her stomach with no more respect for it than if it had been a ferret!"

"I suppose if you drink too much tea——" she helped the wasp on to the edge of the plate with a crust of bread.

"Too much! One cup is too much! Your youthful stomach is probably even now coated with tannin. Dark brown, like the inside of a Victorian infirmary. No wonder your nerves are on edge."

That, Bertie supposed, was a reference to her behaviour at lunch. If he liked to think her criminal tea-drinking was the cause of it, he was welcome. For someone who had kicked the habit, Mrs. Pigeon was looking pretty nervous. The wasp had waded straight back into the molasses.

"Will you have some milk, dear, then?"

"Give her some milk, Mrs. Pigeon, immediately. A girl of her age needs two pints a day. I shall check it in my diet charts, but two pints should be the average, I'm sure. We had better have a consultation on this whole question of Roberta's food, Mrs. Pigeon. Come to my study after tea."

Bertie, drinking the milk after fishing two tiny flies out of it, thought that Mrs. Pigeon didn't look a bit happy about this. She wasn't too happy herself. If the molasses stuff was any sample of what Great-Uncle Felix thought she ought to be eating, she was in for a sticky time. Witty, again, it was a shame Minty wasn't here to get that one. Perhaps she could put it in a letter to her. She could write it after tea.

"And what have you been doing with your time, Roberta? Working, meditating, contemplating nature?"

"I was looking at the garden."

"What did you think of the roses?"

Bertie tried to remember any roses. "They were lovely."

"We only grow the ancient rose. None of your modern hybrids without sense or smell. There is a heraldry of roses, Roberta, a family tree of roses that takes one back to the Crusades. Remind me to show you the book I am writing on roses. I have a number of notes which might interest you."

In some ways, thought Roberta, he doesn't treat me like a child at all, more like another grown-up. It was quite flattering, in a way, but he probably only did it because he was too dotty to notice the difference. She hoped he'd forget about the book on roses, she'd be absolutely stuck for things to say. Perhaps she could have a chat with the gardener about them first, though.

"What's the name of the gardener?"

"Moss. Most appropriate. He's not here today. Comes on Mondays, Tuesdays and Thursdays. Can't afford him all the time, alas. Got to keep an eye on him, too, or he'll sneak one of these weedkillers in. Uses inorganic stuff without any conscience. Ignorant, but he has a way with roses."

So it wasn't the gardener—unless he was busy sneaking in some weedkiller on his day off, which was only a fantasy.

"Were you in the big lawn this afternoon, Uncle Felix?"

"This afternoon? Some more lemon-juice, if you please, Mrs.

Pigeon, we need all the Vitamin C we can get, this summer has not been nearly sunny enough to provide our winter stock. No, I was extremely busy in my study this afternoon. I am working out the precise relationship of John of Gaunt to Charles I."

Bertie had no idea what this called for. She put on the sort of expression Miss Mallors liked when she sat in the front row and got on with drawing ballet dancers in her rough note-book instead of taking notes. It registered vague zeal.

"Sharpens the mind; I must show you my trees some time."

Bertie directed the zeal, even more vaguely, at the woods in the distance.

"In my study, Roberta. I have a number hanging up there and I am hoping to have a few of them illuminated."

*Son et lumière* with Great-Uncle Felix's moustache spot-lit from below. Who on earth could it have been in the garden?

"Is there anybody else round here besides you and Mrs. Pigeon?"

"I have heard of an excellent man who illuminates but, alas, it is far from cheap. The colours alone, hand ground in the correct way, cost a great deal. No, why do you ask?"

For some reason Bertie was reluctant to talk about it. She had recourse to her usual protection.

"Don't mumble, child. I am not deaf, but I cannot stand bad elocution. Look up, speak up! Put that abominable seaweed out of your eyes. Mrs. Pigeon, you must lend her some of the things you stick in your hair to keep all that stuff out of her food."

You can't talk about hair in your food, with that moustache. And no feeble little hairpins can keep back this lot, thought Bertie proudly under the heavy swathes that had defied Miss Mallors' efforts with elastic bands. The one that broke with a dull ping and rocketed across the desks had made a disaster area out of that history lesson. Great-Uncle Felix was looking at her with sharp irritation, and she remembered he was still waiting for an answer.

"I thought I saw someone, that's all."

"Who?"

"Well, if there isn't anyone, I couldn't have."

"No. There is no one to see. Imagination plays a powerful

19

part in what is reflected on the retina, Roberta. You may have seen your imagination in the garden."

For some reason, Great-Uncle Felix seemed to find this funny. He turned his head through an angle of ninety degrees from one to the other, sniggering—there was no other word for it—through his moustache. Mrs. Pigeon had begun to pack up the tea things. There were three wasps up to their elbows in the molasses. Bertie noticed that Mrs. Pigeon didn't attack them but scooped them out deftly and put them to unstick on the edge of the iron table. Great-Uncle Felix watched with approval.

"Man may be at war with the rest of creation, Roberta, but that does not mean he is absolved from the rules of chivalry."

Pride comes before a fall, but never hit an enemy when he's stuck up. I hope I remember all this to tell Minty. Bertie poised herself on the edge of the chair, ready to leave the tea table the moment Great-Uncle Felix got up. In her pocket the stone she had picked up slid with the tilt of her skirt, and she put her hand in to slip her fingers over the shape of it again.

The field beyond Great-Uncle Felix shifted and the woods swam round it. She shut her eyes and shook her head.

"You disagree? You think perhaps such an argument is invalid where the rules are not observed by the other side? On the contrary, that is where the true spirit of chivalry enters."

The field was normal again, and the woods didn't move, but Bertie didn't trust them. There was something funny about everything she looked at, as though the outlines of things hadn't quite settled on top of the things they were outlining; but the effect wasn't blurred at all but too sharp. Somehow, instead of it being just her, looking at the landscape, the landscape was looking back at her. It wasn't a comfortable feeling.

"Are you all right, dear? You're looking rather pale."

Mrs. Pigeon looked like a negative of herself, with light round the edges. The effect only lasted a second, and then Bertie was able to make "I'm fine, don't worry about me" noises.

"You should have rested after the journey, dear, and not run off into the garden in this heat."

"The girl is perfectly well, Mrs. Pigeon, there is nothing wrong with her that an energy diet won't put right. She is simply weak from taking in substances deleterious to her tissues at a time when Nature decrees that she should grow. Take that tray away, and come to my study. I will look out a diet sheet."

"I think she should go early to bed all the same, Mr. Featherstone, and have only a light supper."

"Naturally. Naturally." Great-Uncle Felix looked annoyed. "I would hardly suggest a *heavy* supper. Let her have some yoghurt and wheatgerm, on a tray. That will be sufficiently nourishing."

Whether it was just Mrs. Pigeon and Great-Uncle Felix discussing her like a patient on a slab or what, Bertie suddenly felt both tired out and really cross. If they'd only shut up jawing on about food . . . she was sick of hearing of it. The idea of getting away from them both—even to that mildewed four-poster—was a welcome one. She picked up the breadboard and knife, for which there was no room on the tray, and followed Mrs. Pigeon off the terrace.

The dining-room windows were sash ones, but very long and to the ground, so that it was possible—if you were as short as Mrs. Pigeon or bent your head like Bertie—to step through the open bottom half on to the dining-room parquet. Bertie had no idea where the kitchen was and, after Mrs. Pigeon had bustled before her through several rooms, was no clearer on the subject when they finally reached it. A shy-looking girl got up from the table in a hurry as they came in.

"This is Maudie, dear. She helps me about the house. Have you quite finished, Maudie? Don't rush yourself, dear, because I've got to go to Mr. Featherstone's study for a bit, to have a talk with him, and you can get on with the washing-up in your own time."

Bertie was rather amused to see that on her own ground Mrs. Pigeon wasn't nearly as subdued as she seemed with Great-Uncle Felix; she patted Maudie kindly on the shoulder and pressed her back into her chair in front of her unfinished cup of tea and half-demolished biscuit. Maudie managed to jerk the table edge and upset the tea into her saucer. As she went scarlet and tried to mop it up with her apron, Bertie realised with astonishment that Maudie must be shy of her. She couldn't possibly carry on like that every time Mrs. Pigeon spoke to her. She had brown hair, caught rather wispily into an elastic band at the nape of her slender neck, and a pale, very clear skin. If Great-Uncle Felix sees much of her, thought Bertie, she'll find herself on an energy diet in a brace of molasses. Something occurred to her.

"Does Maudie drink tea, Mrs. Pigeon?"

Maudie, who had succeeded in getting the tea from her saucer back into her cup, slopped it straight out again. Mrs. Pigeon's hands fluttered up to her bun, which had started to shed pins like a hedgehog under stress.

"Yes, dear. Now I must really hurry or I'll keep Mr. Feather-stone waiting—I'll give you your tray, dear, when I come back. You can take it up with you; I know it's just after tea, but you can have it when you feel like it, and go to bed early."

Bertie, left alone with Maudie, felt rather ashamed of herself for asking such a disturbing question. It was really no business of hers if Mrs. Pigeon and Maudie chose to smuggle tea on to the premises and, in any case, she was much more inclined to sympathise with them than with Great-Uncle Felix. If she had to live with a tyrant she might as well join the Resistance Movement. She indicated the cup awkwardly.

"Do carry on. I wish I could join you. I love tea, and I've just had to drink gallons of yukky milk."

Maudie had brown eyes, at the moment rather hopeful. She also had a nice smile, blessed with dimples.

"Do you really like it? Would you like a cup, then? I can easy make some fresh for you. This is all brewed."

"Oh no, don't bother. I don't think I could get any more liquid down . . . Do you help in the garden, too?"

Not that it could have been Maudie, the figure had been far too tall. Funny how she really wanted to know who it could have been, when she wouldn't know him anyway.

"Oh no, Mr. Featherstone wouldn't let me do that. Nor would my uncle—he gardens for Mr. Featherstone, and he says I'd only do the wrong thing. Mr. Featherstone's really fussy about the garden."

"I bet he's fussy about the house too." One part of Bertie told her that she shouldn't criticise her great-uncle to his employee, and the other that it was his own fault if people did. It was nice, too, talking to someone about her own age for a change. "How old are you?"

"Sixteen. I just left school. I'm going to be a nurse, but they won't take me till I'm eighteen, so I'm filling in time here. My uncle told me Mrs. Pigeon wanted an extra hand, and she's very kind. The only thing I really don't like is your uncle—if you don't mind me saying so." Maudie was embarrassed again. "I mean, I expect he's awfully nice really, as a person and all that, and I know he's very clever, but he scares the life out of me, he does, honestly. He's just like Mr. Thursdon who used to teach wood-work, the boys all said he sawed up the ones he didn't like and used them for bookends." Maudie giggled engagingly. "But Mrs. Pigeon, she's teaching me a lot more about cooking than I ever learnt in Domestic Science. Her food is really nice, too." Maudie seemed to warm to her confidences and lose some of her shyness, and Bertie felt a touch of envy. If *she* had known something about nursing, she wouldn't have been packed off here, she could have looked after Daddy properly. But she mustn't think of any of that. Maudie, who looked a lot more competent now one knew about the nursing, was emptying out the tea-leaves, saying, "I make a proper pig of myself over Mrs. Pigeon's cooking."

"Isn't cooking here a bit funny? I mean, my great-uncle's a bit faddy about his food, isn't he? I bet you don't get a chance to make steamed pud, or pies, and so on. He seems frightfully against anything that isn't practically raw."

Maudie looked sly. She began to collect the plates off the tray and put them in the sink.

"Well, we practise things, but Mr. Featherstone doesn't have them always, see."

Bertie thought she did. Great-Uncle Felix's moustache would fall off with sheer horror if it knew what was going on right under it in the back kitchen. Still, this did seem as though she could get a little sustaining food, and, of course, tea from the guerrilla troops any time she really felt she couldn't stand the molasses treatment a moment longer.

"You here for a long stay?" Maudie obviously wanted to change the subject, but the new one was not one Bertie cared for.

"Not very long, I expect." And hope, she added silently.

Maudie was working up to her elbows in a sea of detergent. "I heard about your father. I'm ever so sorry."

What on earth did you say when people said things like that? Did you thank them for being sorry, or what? Bertie did, felt an idiot, and hated Maudie for making her feel one. She wanted to get out of the kitchen, away from everybody. A happy thought came to her.

"I haven't unpacked yet. I'd better go up and do that."

When Bertie got outside the kitchen, she remembered that she hadn't the slightest idea of where her room was. In this house, half the rooms seemed to lead into one another, instead of opening on to corridors which gave you a glimpse of where you were going. Still, if she kept right on, she'd be bound to come to that slippery staircase, and from there she knew the way.

The rooms she went through were high-ceilinged, and dark because of the panelling which covered the walls, and the deep brown velvet of the chair-coverings. Great-Uncle Felix seemed to like the colour. Perhaps it reminded him of molasses. The windows were quite big, however, and held views of the garden in the evening sun beyond, like coloured slides held up to the light. There was a window-seat in one room that she promised herself she'd come back to and curl up in sometime.

She saw the staircase in the hall beyond the room she was in, just when she'd thought that perhaps Great-Uncle Felix's study was one of the rooms she would have to go through before she came to it.

In thinking there were no corridors, she'd forgotten the one at the top of the stairs leading to her room, which had such a tilt to it that she arrived in a sort of run that the slope of her floor to the window did nothing to check.

Later, after she had washed and unpacked, and the tray Mrs. Pigeon had made Maudie bring up was sitting on the table by the bed, she knelt on the chair in front of the low window to look out once more at the garden before she got into bed. On the window-sill was the chipped stone she had picked up in the garden. She fingered it dreamily as she looked out into the twilight.

There was Great-Uncle Felix crossing the lawn. She began to move back into the room, but something made her stop. He was wearing a fringed jacket and his hair fell to his shoulders. It was certainly not Great-Uncle Felix.

# CHAPTER

4

She wondered at breakfast whether or not to tell Great-Uncle Felix that he had trespassers; or at least a trespasser. It wasn't anything world-shaking, after all, but the idea of someone unknown wandering about the garden—it must have been the same one she had seen earlier on, as well—was somehow unsettling. She hadn't any silly ideas about burglars. He certainly wasn't dressed like a burglar, but then perhaps she wasn't in touch with the right thing for a modern burglar to wear. She didn't really think he would jump out and attack her. All the same, he had looked so absurdly at home crossing the lawn last night that she felt Great-Uncle Felix had a right to know.

"There was a young man wandering about the garden yesterday. I saw him twice."

"There couldn't have been, dear." Mrs. Pigeon seemed puzzled. "There isn't anyone who could have. You must have imagined it."

"When did you think you saw him, Roberta?"

"Last night. I thought it was you at first."

"Was it getting dark?"

"It was sort of twilight."

"Precisely." Great-Uncle Felix stuffed a piece of egg under his moustache with a satisfied air.

Bertie felt furious. She wasn't half-blind and she didn't go around dreaming things.

"The first time I saw him was broad daylight."

"Where was he?"

"Coming out of that big lawn place with the hedge round it."

"Did you see this clearly?"

"Not really. He was the other side."

"In the shadow?"

"I suppose so."

"A trick of the sun, Roberta. Not unusual. It has even happened to me. You blink your eyes, the sun dazzles, and a figure seems to move in the distance. When I was your age I was living here under somewhat lonely circumstances. I used to take advantage of that trick of the eyes, and pretend that I had a companion. It is amazing how easy it is to deceive oneself if one wishes."

"He was wearing long hair and a fringed jacket. He looked hippie."

"When I was your age I thought of that as a Robin Hood figure. Extraordinary how fashion perverts the imagination." Great-Uncle Felix polished his moustache with his table-napkin which he then laid by his plate. A thought seemed to strike him. "It might, of course, have been young Pack. I told him he could come round at any time he wanted and look over the grounds— though I hardly see the point of his going through the gardens. We don't want him excavating the rose-bed."

Great-Uncle Felix found this very funny, and treated them to his revolving snigger, with his head turning like a conning tower above the machine-gunning moustache. Who was young Pack, Roberta wondered.

"The Packs, Roberta, are our neighbours. They are the owners of the farmhouse about a mile from here. Archaeologists, both of them; they have a boy and girl a bit older than you, I think; Gawain and Clothilde."

"No," said Bertie, awed.

"Yes, indeed. Most ill-advised, I agree. But they are both confident young people and seem to have survived the mockery of their contemporaries without obvious scarring."

"I don't think I've ever heard of anything more ghastly."

"Romantic, romantic rather than ghastly, but youth is not romantic. Contrary to what most people believe, Mrs. Pigeon, the young are practical. If we do not think so it is merely that their techniques are at fault. My own first name, Roberta, was one I sought to conceal when I was young."

Impossible that Great-Uncle Felix could ever have been so young. Bertie couldn't imagine that moustache not grey, let alone that face without a moustache. Even as a baby, he must have had one.

"What was it, Uncle Felix?"

"Was! Is. I'm still alive, Roberta, and my name, as I do not hesitate to announce now, is Lancelot."

Bertie's mouth quivered, and then, without planning it any more than she would plan a sneeze, she burst out laughing. Luckily, Uncle Felix seemed to be gratified, if anything, by her reaction, though Mrs. Pigeon looked a bit alarmed.

"Exactly. Lancelot Felix Featherstone. None of my contemporaries know that it stood for anything worse than Leonard. I took care of that. But I do not think that Clothilde and Gawain Pack, as I say, suffer unduly from their names. They appear well set-up in their own esteem."

Bertie interpreted this as 'stuck-up' and was sorry. For a moment she had almost felt cheerful at the idea of two people her own age not far away, who might prove more sparkling conversationalists than Maudie in the kitchen. Great-Uncle Felix had finished his wholemeal toast and molasses and was dry-cleaning his moustache with his napkin.

"I have to go over that way today, to see Marling about the ha-ha. You had better come with me in the car, and I'll drop you off at the Packs' place on the way and you can make their acquaintance. They can talk to you about their hobby, which is at least an intelligent one."

Bertie felt far from comfortable. A stuck-up boy and his sister, older than she, who would talk to her about something she didn't know anything about—it would have been a lot nicer to stay at home and wander about the gardens again. She didn't, however, fancy putting this to Great-Uncle Felix who was, in any case, getting up and dusting down his elderly tweed jacket which, in spite of the napkin, had a carpet of toast crumbs on it.

"I shall be ready in half an hour. Do not keep me waiting, Roberta."

She did keep him waiting, in fact, as she wanted to make sure that she didn't look too ghastly for Clothilde—it really was un-believable—to laugh at. Older than she was mighṫ mean more make-up or something. Bertie made up her eyes very carefully and, for once, took a little time over brushing her hair. She was doing that when she thought part of the house had blown up and was coming unsteadily round the corner. She ran to the window and saw an awful old car shuddering and going off like a firecracker in the drive. Great-Uncle Felix was sitting in it, look-ing at his watch.

She was getting quite used to skidding on the corners by now, and luckily it wasn't too hard to locate the front door, which was opposite the stairs, and open.

"It isn't half an hour yet!"

"Nevertheless, you have kept me waiting, you see."

He let in the clutch with a satisfied expression and they boun-ded urgently forward. Bertie was sitting with her mouth open, after the blinding unfairness of what Great-Uncle Felix had said, and she felt it click shut of itself, like a toy. The mother of one of her friends, Jane, took them out for drives sometimes when she stayed in the country with them, and she used to call the kind of driving they were doing now 'using kangaroo petrol'. Great-Uncle Felix seemed not disturbed by it, however. He looked per-fectly serene as they leapt towards the gate, and greeted the road outside with a proud fanfare on the horn. And if they know what's good for them, Bertie thought, they'll take notice.

It was about twenty minutes' drive to the Packs' cottage, but it was a hair-raising twenty minutes. Great-Uncle Felix discoursed about the view, he turned round to look at things they had passed, he pointed at things they were passing, he peered with his moustache on a level with the wheel to observe the things they were going, with any luck, to pass. Everything else on the road had to find its way round him, and Bertie noticed with relief that they did. Perhaps on this road, it was mostly B roads that they followed, people knew his car. If they had seen it once, after all, they would hardly forget it. Some who had only seen it once, on their way to London or something, might still be waking in the middle of the night, screaming.

29

The Packs' cottage looked rather pretty, with a clematis flower-
ing purple round the doorway, just like something out of a Milly-
Molly-Mandy picture. There was a huge barn-like building behind
it, and some trees partly sheltering it from the road. The car
came to an exploding halt outside, and Bertie, when she had
picked herself off the windscreen, was not surprised to see a head
peering from a front window. A large man came hurrying through
the little front garden.

"Featherstone, I didn't expect you. Come in, come in."

The big brown face, bent to look in at the window, was covered
in little fine seams, like an American Indian's, and the eyes were
inky dark but quite friendly.

"Can't, my dear fellow." Great-Uncle Felix waved an airy
hand. "On my way to discuss the ha-ha, thought I'd drop my
niece here, Roberta, meet your young people. Call for her on my
way back."

When put to it, he could communicate in quite rapid tele-
graphese. Bertie didn't really relish being dumped like a sack of
potatoes, and she wasn't a bit looking forward to Gawain and
Clothilde, but Mr. Pack—she supposed it was Mr. Pack—came
and held the door for her to get out just as though she were
grown up. It was a pity she had to catch her shoe on one of the
tears in the rubber mat on the floor, and come out head-first,
almost knocking him over. Great-Uncle Felix completed the Marx
Brothers effect by shooting forward and making both her and Mr.
Pack jump out of the way. Bertie saw the airy hand waving
to them out of the window as the car detonated down the
road.

"Known as the Banger." Mr. Pack put his hands in the pockets
of his windcheater and smiled down at her. "I imagine that anything that tried to tangle with it would certainly become Mash.
Enter and meet my young."

He was really too tall for his cottage, and he made the passage-
way to the back living-room look very uncomfortable. Bertie
found herself cramping her shoulders as she followed, quite un-
necessarily. The walls had rather a damp smell, and the living-
room, which was also, she saw, a kitchen, smelt old and a bit
neglected as well. In the middle of the jumble of furniture two

30

leggy creatures sprawled, both in jeans, both looking up from their books under black fringes with much the same kind of arrogant caution.

"This is Gawain." Mr. Pack's blunt finger indicated the one lying on the end of his spine on the sagging sofa. "This is Clothilde." The other one, as Bertie now saw, shipwrecked in the huge basket-chair, wore glasses and was female. Neither of them said anything. "And this is Roberta, Mr. Featherstone's niece. He'll be back for her shortly."

And, with this parting consolation all round, he nodded and left them. Bertie felt like an early Christian thrown to the camels. It was amazing how people could look down their noses at you, even though you were standing and they were sitting down.

"Are you going to be here long?" It was the male one who asked, and his voice was even more supercilious than his face.

"As long as it takes." Bertie felt a certain wild coolness descend on her.

"What takes?" The female was faintly interested.

"My cure."

Gawain sat up, which he managed by feeding his spine up the back of the sofa. "You ill or something?"

"Going to drop off any minute?" Clothilde sounded as though she would quite like to witness this.

"Perhaps." Bertie affected a great nonchalance and, seeing they weren't going to offer her a chair, sank into the nearest and waved her hand rather like Great-Uncle Felix. "Who knows what will happen?"

Gawain and Clothilde contemplated this for a minute.

"Who, indeed," he agreed gravely. "What's wrong with you?"

"I'm not supposed to tell people, but it isn't infectious, so don't worry."

"We're not. Are you on alcohol or drugs?"

Bertie was at a loss for a moment. She had been delighted to hold her own like this before the dreaded Packs, but a cold splash of reality was more than she had bargained for. She wasn't sure whether Clothilde thought she really could be an alcoholic or an addict but, of course, she supposed she might be. A girl had got expelled from school for taking drugs, Jane had been offered some at a party, people her age *were* addicts. But it wasn't a joke, she wanted to say. Instead, she dropped her eyes and twisted the ring she had put on, a huge fake pearl stuck on a black plastic band.

"I'm not allowed to say. It's part of the cure."

She saw Clothilde was looking at the ring, and was pleased. Minty said it was vulgar, but at the moment that was how she wanted to be.

"What does it matter, anyway, it's her business." Gawain got up and dropped his book on the sofa. "She's a leper, so she's tinkled her bell. We can't complain."

"What school do you go to?"

"Morven High. What do you?"

"St. Barnabas."

And that, thought Bertie, was that. Game, set and match. Jane had been to St. Barnabas Junior and had told her about the Senior School, where she had gone to fail her entrance examination. It was all wood panelling and glass partitions, gilded organs—one, anyway—oil paintings of former headmistresses, names of scholars in gold leaf on the walls. Morven High would seem like a kind of intellectual slum to Clothilde.

"What do you do when you're staying with your uncle?"

Bertie repressed the reply that she had only been staying with him for two days so she hadn't found out yet, and she also stopped herself saying "Just mucking about" which was her second idea and was, no doubt, all they thought she was capable of. Something Great-Uncle Felix had said came back into her mind.

"Writing a book, actually."

This time their eyes really opened. Inky, like their father's.

"A book? Do you mean a diary?"

"Oh no, a book. Anyone can write a diary."

"But it takes Boswell or Pepys to write a diary that's worth publishing. What's it about?"

By now they must know she was bluffing—how could someone her age be writing a book, or, at least, a book anyone would publish?—but Bertie was grimly determined to keep up her bluff, particularly when she looked at the curl of Gawain's lip.

"Oh, about Longbarrow, of course. I'm drawing on Uncle Felix's records and things."

"Of course." For a moment Gawain's eyes held hers, and then he smiled, quite nicely. "Perhaps Rupert could help. He knows quite a lot about the country round here, and naturally Longbarrow is quite a landmark."

So Gawain had decided to accept her bluff as a kind of joke. Bertie was pleased; she even felt she had passed a kind of test.

"Rupert?"

"Our father." Clothilde didn't look as though she found Bertie's joke quite so amusing. There was something definitely hostile in the flash of her spectacles as she turned an unsmiling face. "Rupert Pack. He's fairly well known as an archaeologist."

They were just the sort of children who would call their father by his Christian name, if only to confuse people. She hoped they wouldn't carry her joke too far, and tell either their father or, horrors, Great-Uncle Felix. To exorcise the idea, she jumped up and began to roam around the room.

"What on earth are these?"

On the long, scrubbed wooden table that was evidently used both as a place to study and somewhere to eat—there was a large book with a spoon to mark the place—were about six pointed flaky stones, just like the one she had picked up in the garden yesterday. To make quite sure, she brought it out from her pocket and held it beside them. The table waltzed briefly and was still.

"Hallo, are you all right?" Gawain's hand was under her elbow. She wondered what she had looked like.

"I'm fine. Just felt a bit dizzy."

Now Clothilde was peering at her. "You look a bit funny. Where did you get that?" Her gaze had transferred to the stone. "Nice specimen. Rupert'd like that, wouldn't he, Gawain?"

"Super. Let's have a look."

Bertie found her hand closing tightly over the stone so that the sharp flakes bit into her fingers. She had to make herself relax and hand it over. Absurd, as if Gawain were going to steal it or something—as if it mattered, anyway.

But it was Clothilde who put out her hand and took it. She held it for a moment and then placed it carefully on the table,

33

took off her glasses and polished them on the tail of her jersey. In that second Bertie knew for a certainty that she, too, had felt that strange disturbance of sight that had come to her from the stone. For it was the stone that altered her seeing, but it was only watching Clothilde that made her admit it to herself for the first time.

Gawain took up the stone and turned it appreciatively in his hand.

"Wonder how many Neolithic dinners this fellow nailed— Hallo, who's that?"

"Who's what?"

"At the window. Peering in at us."

"Probably someone looking for Rupert."

As Gawain pushed past to the door, Bertie's hand came out and took the stone from his. It seemed important that it should come back to her, and she put it quickly in her pocket out of the way of other hands than hers.

"What did he mean about dinner?"

"Well, it looks as if it would make quite an efficient sort of an arrow, doesn't it? Rupert says there are quite a number round here, must have been a kind of factory in Neolithic times."

"The silly thing is, it's no good asking people round here if they've seen any, because they're still considered unlucky." Gawain had rejoined them, and was fidgeting with Mr. Pack's specimens on the table, rearranging them with their points the same way. Clothilde walked away, her bored voice trailing over her shoulder.

"They're a bunch of peasants anyway, still living in the Dark Ages. It's no good telling them they're Neolithic arrowheads. *They* call them elfstones, and think they cast charms, stop cows giving milk, bewitch people and things like that. Who was it, Gawain?"

"No idea. Whoever it was, he'd gone by the time I got outside. Jolly fast, too, because there was no one in sight, even."

Bertie was silent. He had crossed the lawn yesterday evening. Today he had looked in at the window. Perhaps the next time she would see him properly, and, although she was frightened, she was also aware that she wanted that time to come. Wherever he came from, it was the stone that brought him.

# CHAPTER

## 5

These thoughts passed through her mind before she noticed what she was thinking; when she did she gave herself a mental shake. Living with Great-Uncle Felix only two days had already put the skids under her trolley if she was imagining there was some kind of *magic* going on. She hardly wanted to be one of the bunch of peasants Clothilde was talking about, babbling about elfstones—*elf*stones!—and spells. There was, no doubt, a perfectly ordinary explanation for everything,—and there wasn't much to explain, anyway. She probably *wasn't* quite well, after all the ghastly things that had happened at home, which would easily account for the dizziness, and as for the face at the window, why shouldn't it have been someone for Mr. Pack? A quick walker, though, impossibly quick, prompted the other, credulous side of her that she was surprised to find existed—and what about Clothilde putting the elfstone down and cleaning her glasses? So they were dirty, replied her rational side.

A noise like a couple of dustbins having a catfight outside announced the arrival of Great-Uncle Felix. It appeared the man he wanted to discuss the ha-ha with—and Bertie couldn't help visualising them, when they did meet to discuss it, sitting opposite one another with balloons coming out of their heads, labelled 'Ha-ha'—was not in, and Great-Uncle Felix was fussing away to Mr. Pack about people forgetting appointments.

"It was really most important I should get that ha-ha strengthened before any autumn rains. It's amazing how little one can trust people nowadays. They seem to have no conception of duty to others."

"Have you decided yet about letting us dig, Mr. Featherstone?" Gawain was leaning nonchalantly against the sofa, juggling two of his father's flint arrowheads. Bertie got the impression, as her great-uncle turned a slightly indignant moustache towards him, that this was somehow an important question, and Mr. Pack, from his uncomfortable expression, would not have asked the question himself just yet.

"That's not a matter to be decided in a hurry, young man. Serious considerations enter into it. For you, it's just poking about for curiosity's sake——"

"A good definition of archaeology," murmured Mr. Pack pleasantly from his bulky height, and was ignored both by his son and Great-Uncle Felix who were facing one another like opponents in a duel.

"——Curiosity's sake, but I have to think of my land. And of preserving traditions, of course. Not only that," Great-Uncle Felix raised a hand in a singularly irritating fashion, as of one who quells a quick reply, though Gawain had shown no sign of making one, "not only that, but I have to think of my own plans for the future, you know. I must think of my Folly."

Bertie was wanting terribly to laugh until she saw from Gawain's expression that he wanted to, too, and she was surprised at the fierce surge of family feeling that stiffened her face and killed the laughter. She looked angrily at Clothilde to see if she were smiling, but she simply wore her usual bored look.

"A Folly is a great responsibility. I can hardly find a better place for it in the whole grounds. It is an eminence, and it would be absurd not to take advantage of it."

"But is the mound in the best place for the Folly?"

Great-Uncle Felix hesitated, and Bertie thought: the father can handle this better than the son.

"Perhaps not, perhaps not. There should be a better vista from the house, I agree. But that need only be a matter of cutting down a few trees, clearing the way a bit. It could be arranged."

The lines on Mr. Pack's face had taken on a bloodhound sadness. Great-Uncle Felix seemed positively stimulated by the idea of arranging a vista, whatever that was. Spaniards, she knew, from a book she had picked up once, were always saying 'Hasta la vista' to each other, but as she only knew 'hasta' as a spear in Latin, she had seen them raising their spears at each other in a gesture rather like shaking a fist.

"You do realise that this could be a Bronze Age find of the first importance?" Clothilde, standing behind Gawain, echoed his expression of irritated condescension.

"Bronze Age rubbish! A few bones and a clumsy necklace or two, hardly worth the designing. And where will they go? Into a glass case in some museum, where nobody will look at them." He swivelled his moustache triumphantly. Mr. Pack, still with his hands in his pockets, sank his head a little further between his broad shoulders. If the father looked like an American Indian with indigestion, the son and daughter looked merely exasperated. Gawain actually didn't sound bored.

"You can hardly dismiss an important contribution of know-ledge——"

"Important contribution of fiddlesticks! Young man, you have absolutely no idea of what I can or cannot dismiss. Roberta, we must be going." The bony hands were gripped hard on the edges of his ancient mackintosh and Bertie suddenly understood that he was genuinely upset and, going over to join him at the door, glared at Gawain from her defensive position. Mr. Pack moved forward to block out the view of his furious offspring, ush-ering Bertie and Great-Uncle Felix outside to the car.

"I'm sorry you feel that way, Featherstone, but I'm sure you can understand that we all feel very strongly about it, just as you do, of course. Don't let's take this as a final decision, we'll have another little chat about it some time . . . Perhaps I could come up one day and see your plans for the Folly? I'd be very inter-ested to see what you intend."

Great-Uncle Felix was mollified. "Of course, my dear fellow, at any time. I think you'll be surprised at my blend of styles. Classi-cal but daring, you know." He waved his hand out of the car window. "Of course you must come up and see the plans. It'll be a nice change for you."

From his children, from archaeology? Bertie wondered, and was shot forward the next instant by the car's insane progress down the road. A volley of hoots behind them told her that her great-uncle had succeeded in maddening a few more people in addition to the Packs.

"Pompous young ass! Trying to instruct me in my own business!"

"I don't suppose he could understand about your Folly." Bertie, enjoying the other meaning of what she was saying, was surprised both at her treachery and at that instinct which makes one defend whomever is being attacked at the time, regardless of what side one was on last. How often she had suffered from this switching of sides in the past, and how painful it was to see, first, her mother's point of view, and then her father's.

"I expect you are right, Roberta." The bony hands relaxed on the wheel. "I cannot really expect a boy of that kind, clearly without aesthetic sensitivity or he wouldn't dabble about with those unsophisticated gewgaws, to appreciate my Folly. His father, however, is not quite such a fool. He is willing to learn, you notice. ROADHOG!"

Bertie, startled, realised that this ferocious scream was addressed not to the absent Mr. Pack but to the man in the red car who, after vainly attempting to get past them in a narrow road, had seized the opportunity of a sudden widening to escape from their frightful back view. Great-Uncle Felix punched his horn with evident enjoyment, but with rather unnerving effect on the steering. After they had wandered violently towards and away from the verge a couple of times, he resumed the conversation.

"You must come to my study after lunch for your diet-sheet. I have already given one to Mrs. Pigeon, but it is as well you should have a copy too; and then I can show you the Folly plans."

Bertie's stomach shrank at the thought of this study visit, but then she remembered the two ghastly lies she had already involved herself in with the Packs—it was amazing how some people made you say things you didn't want to say, drew them out of you against your will simply by sitting there and waiting for you to speak. If she were to justify in any way the idiotic things she had said about being on a cure, and writing a book on Longbarrow, then the diet sheet and the plans for the Folly were designed to support both lies, and even though the Packs were unlikely to see either (barring Chief Silvertongue, that is) it somehow might make her feel less guilty. Anyway, there were a lot of things that needed explaining, and perhaps Great-Uncle Felix would explain. She wasn't entirely sure what a Folly was, though she knew it was a sort of building, and as for the mound on which it was to be built, she hadn't even noticed that yet; but perhaps it wasn't near the garden but just on Featherstone land somewhere, because the fields round the house and garden all belonged to ᵗhe estate, her mother had told her.

Thoughts of her mother made her suddenly miserable again. What was happening at her grandmother's? Why did she have to be here, with this loony great-uncle, wasting her time doing nothing when she might have been helping her mother? At least she could have taken some of her grandmother's attention off her mother, and saved her a bit of that gentle pestering. Goodness knows she'd be a lot worse with Daddy ill, probably telling Mother exactly how to look after him and behaving as though Mother wasn't a grown-up at all or knew anything about anything. It was funny listening to Grandmother and realising that from the way she talked to Mother she obviously thought of her as being much the same age group as Bertie herself. Probably Great-Uncle Felix would do the same, if he got a chance to talk to Mother— but one nice thing about him at least was that he seemed totally to forget what age-group Bertie was in at all, and it was a pleasant change after the teachers at school telling her things with that exasperated 'dear' tacked on at the end, as though people of her age were mentally deficient.

"SLOWCOACH !" The words bellowed into her ear nearly lifted her hair off. Great-Uncle Felix was leaning forward, with glittering eyes staring beyond her at a car driven by a meek-looking elderly woman. Their own car, goaded into a dangerous forty-five miles an hour, banged palpitatingly ahead as they overtook.

"A rabbit like that shouldn't be allowed on the road. Dodderers cause accidents."

To her horror, Bertie began to cry again. This time, luckily, she was silent, and Great-Uncle Felix was too busy admiring in

39

the driving-mirror the distance he was putting between himself and the overtaken rabbit to notice.

Unfortunately, though, his statement had reminded him of the one thing Bertie wanted not to discuss.

"How's your father, then? Funny thing, concussion, fell off a horse when I was a child, couldn't see straight for a week. Kept walking into things." He seemed to find the memory amusing, and Bertie, trying to sniff quietly—why did one's *nose* have to run as well as one's eyes?—hoped he would forget his original question. "Of course, a couple of broken ribs are neither here nor there. Strap 'em up and take plenty of exercise. Never make the mistake of thinking, when people want you to rest, that you mustn't exercise. Arabella's probably got your father tied to the bed, always had as much sense as a pie-witted hen."

This description of her grandmother was curiously soothing, and Bertie was grateful at being able to turn a hearty sniff into something resembling a laugh. She shook her hair further over her face to disguise the tearmarks (worse on the make-up she had put on to impress Clothilde, why had she bothered with that mascara?) but Great-Uncle Felix was bringing them into the home run with another burst on the horn as they turned in at the gate.

"That, over there, Roberta, is the mound. Behind the house. It is, of course, what gives the house its name, as those ludicrous Packs would inform you, 'barrow' is the term used for a certain kind of grave mound. Longbarrow itself has stood for a mere four hundred years, the barrow more like four thousand."

Bertie gazed at the mound as she got out of the car, her mind spinning at what she had heard. Of course she had seen it, but had just thought of it as a low hill, with the trees behind it. Now she looked more carefully, she could see it was extraordinarily regular in shape for a natural hill. It was quite some way from the house, about half as long as tall, and sloping slightly to a neat, flat top. She hoped there was time to explore before lunch.

Great-Uncle Felix, echoing her thoughts, waved a hand in its direction.

"Go ahead and get acquainted, Roberta. Later you must tell me what you think of its possibilities for the Folly. Try the view in every direction. Kindly remember that luncheon will be in half an hour. I am not sure you should not rest after luncheon, you have very dark shadows under the eyes."

Bertie didn't wait for him to find out about the mascara but set off at a run for the Knowe. It was lovely feeling her feet race over the grass and her hair lift off her face, after the vibration and leathery smell of the car.

The Knowe was further away than she had thought, and she had to slow down and walk for quite a bit, panting, till she came up to it. It seemed, in its way, to come to meet her, its presence advancing as she advanced, till, once she had stopped and was gazing up at it, it stood over her. The sides were covered in rough grass which shivered in the breeze like the muscles along an animal's back when it twitches at a fly. Four thousand years old. Great-Uncle Felix must have got it wrong. Perhaps she could ask the Packs,—if she ever got a chance to see them again, after that little tiff this morning.

She leant forward and put her hands against the sides of the Knowe. It felt warm and living, just like an animal. What was inside? Great-Uncle Felix had spoken contemptuously of bones and necklaces, and said it was a grave mound. Some grave. But perhaps it was a mass burial, they did have things like that in prehistoric times, quite cheerful, really, being buried with a lot of other people for company, though she had an uneasy memory of being told some of the people didn't always choose to be buried at the same time as someone important, and it was rather decided for them. She moved her hands in the grass on the earth hot from the sun, and turned suddenly to look back at the house. From here it seemed quite small, but cosy, somehow, very much as though it had people living in it. A thin wreath of smoke rose from one of the barley-sugarstick chimneys, probably it was the kitchen where Mrs. Pigeon was getting on with the lunch, with Maudie helping her. Great-Uncle Felix would be fooling around in his study somewhere. And out here, where she was, a great hill full of the dead, and she had her hands on it. She put them into her pockets quickly.

The music was so far away at first that it seemed to be the wind blowing in her ears, and then it grew stronger. It was very sweet, yet almost too shrill to be sweet, like a violin when your nerves were on edge. It seemed to be coming from near at hand now, perhaps the other side of the Knowe. Her mind flew to the young man she had seen twice already. Could it be him, with a transistor? She bent forward, listening intently to locate the sound, in her concentration gripping the stone in her pocket harder.

The music was coming from inside the Knowe.

# CHAPTER
## 6

The part of Bertie that was sure the stone was something not quite of this world accepted that music could come out of a hill, the other, frightened, part urged on her that she was absurdly mistaken, and tried to find a reason for her mistake. It made her walk round the Knowe to find the person who must have the transistor. If there were anyone, he was walking faster than she was, away from her. Something of desperation seized her, and she began to run, clumsily, more as though she were being pursued than pursuing. As if to prove the idiocy of her ideas, the part in her that clung to the ordinary had made her bring the stone out of her pocket and hold it before her as she ran.

She wasn't really surprised when she twisted her foot on a stone and fell. She seemed, as sometimes happens when one is falling, to take a long time over it, time to criticise the silliness of running, time to wonder if she were going to hurt herself, before she struck the earth with a thump that knocked the breath out of her. She lay for an almost peaceful minute or two, not wanting to get up and go through the business of finding out how bad the grazes and bruises were that she must have collected. The grass stems in front of her were like a miniature world; as a child she would lie like this for hours peering through them and shrinking herself to the scale of the insects going about among them.

The stone was lying just ahead of her; it must have jerked out of her hand when she fell. Without thinking, she stretched her

43

hand out to take it again. As she touched it, she saw beyond it a foot.

If she did not move now, it was because nightmare had gripped her. She was sure, she *knew*, that foot had not been there a second ago.

She was still holding the stone, almost in the state of coma of a wild animal taken out of its burrow, when hands gently but firmly helped her to stand. Except that she could not stand. The pain of her twisted ankle made her collapse again, while the figure that stood before her danced and swam with the landscape. Then it was kneeling, and the hands that had helped her to rise were kneading and massaging the swollen ankle she had stuck out stiffly before her. She fixed her eyes on the hands, not believing what they were doing—how could anyone dare to press his fingers into that agonising swelling?—not believing in the hands.

"That will be better now, you will find."

The voice was soft, distant, yet near, as though she were hearing it inside her head. The eyes turned to hers were clear and empty of expression.

"Where did you come from? I didn't see you——" Even her own voice sounded funny, not like her own.

"I did not come from anywhere. I was here all the time."

"But you suddenly appeared——"

"Ah, that," he smiled and touched the stone in her hand. His voice was stronger now, but still in her head. "You have the Opener."

Just as though he were a tin or something. Part of Bertie that had been dazed was beginning to come to the surface again, but she still felt unreal.

"I don't understand what is happening——"

"Understanding is not needed."

He was still crouched on his heels, still smiling at her. Whatever world she was in, he looked at ease in his, yet his face was a sad one.

"Was it you I saw before?"

"If you had that, yes. It has its work."

She looked at the stone in her hand, flaked, shiny, and warm in the sunlight. Neolithic arrowhead, indeed. It would be nice to have Clothilde there at this moment, and watch her eyes bug behind her spectacles.

"Why? I mean, why me?"

"They want to see you. I have been sent."

Things were getting more confusing, not less, yet she had the feeling, which she sometimes got when she was trying to solve a problem in maths, that the solution was there, staring her in the face, if she could only see it. She knew quite well what he was talking about, but she wasn't in touch with the person in her who knew.

"Who are they?"

"They are not spoken of." He was calm, but definite.

She tried another question. "Why send *you*?"

"They think I may remember how to speak to you." The smile had gone now. It was a very sad face, and involuntarily she felt pity, though she didn't know what for.

"Why do they want you to speak to me?"

"So that I may tell you that they wish to see you."

This was going in circles, all right.

"What do they want to see me about?"

"They will tell you that themselves."

"When?" She had been trying every question, almost at random, and this one produced an answer she could recognise, but brought with it a thrill of alarm. He had raised his eyes again and was looking at her intently.

"To-night. You must come here at midnight, alone. Then they will speak to you and tell you what you must know."

"But that's impossible!" She heard her voice rise to a squeak. "I can't possibly come out here at night!"

"Why not? *You*," he emphasised the word, "are not a prisoner."

She searched wildly in her mind for excuses while the expressionless eyes went on looking at her. She wasn't a coward, but really——

"I daresay they lock up the place at night and everything."

Once more he touched the stone in her hand. "Did I not say it was an Opener?"

45

And it was no good saying she didn't believe it, when she did. If she didn't believe it, she didn't believe in him, either, and that seemed, facing him, as much bad manners as anything. He was getting up now, looking down at her quite gravely, his fringed leather jacket patterning the blue sky in silhouette.

"Be here before midnight—and take all the care you may."

The outline of the fringed jacket was less distinct, blurring on the blue of the sky. She grasped the stone tightly with both hands, convinced there was something important he hadn't said.

"What care? What do you mean?"

He bent to put his hand on the stone again, and as his face approached hers, he spoke, swift and low, more like the rustle of the wind in the grass than anything.

"Take nothing that they offer, or you will regret it." The stone was taken out of her grasp by strong fingers unplaiting hers, and dropped at her feet. As it left her hands she protested wordlessly but in that moment the hand taking it was gone, his shadow vanished between her and the sun, and only the stone remained, in the grass where it had fallen.

For a little time, perhaps ten minutes, she stayed, crouched there, without touching the stone. It was restful to go into a kind of daze, much better than thinking about what had happened or what she had to do. If she sat there long enough, it might never have happened, perhaps. The sun shone down on her, hot with noon, the rough coat of the Knowe was parted by the breeze this way and that, and the grass bent and whispered all round her. It was the voice of the grass that brought her back, and reminded her, "Take nothing that they offer . . ."

She shook her head abruptly and scrambled to her feet. It must be lunch time, probably after, and Great-Uncle Felix had warned her not to be late. Laughable he might be, but she wasn't particularly keen to annoy him, Great-Uncle Felix angry with her might not be a bit amusing. She set off for the house at a kind of run. There was a tenderness, if she tried to feel for it, in the ankle she had twisted, but it was miraculous just how it didn't hurt. Not much good in making it an excuse for being late, as she had half thought of doing—there didn't even seem to be any swelling left.

46

She deliberately put out of her mind the thought of those hands.

She was not late for lunch, as it happened, and Great-Uncle Felix, so far from being cross, seemed in an exceptionally genial mood, breaking seaweed crackers ("excellent for the complexion") into his barley soup, and urging her with quite a flattering attention to her opinion to tell him what she thought of the Knowe as a site for the Folly.

"Just the right elevation and view, don't you think? One must take a number of factors into account, you know. The *feel* of the place must take first priority."

Bertie dipped a spoon into her soup and thought of the Knowe and the music coming from it, from under its shaggy hide.

"I didn't think it had the right feel at all."

Great-Uncle Felix was almost comically taken aback. Cracker in knuckly hand, he stared at her like a bereft baby.

"Not the right feel, Roberta?"

"Well," it was impossible to explain what she really meant by it, "it would be undignified, somehow."

Great-Uncle Felix supped his soup noisily, considering the idea.

"Possibly, possibly. It may indeed be too near the house, in too familiar a position, as it were, to have any real consequence. To call my Folly lacking in dignity would be a serious charge to bring against it."

Bertie realised, to her relief, that of course he hadn't understood that it was the presence of the Knowe itself which might be offended by some purposely trivial building dumped on it. She had an uncomfortable vision of its rough shoulders not just twitching the grasses in the wind, but shifting irritably so that the building on top—her idea of the Folly itself was very vague, like a summerhouse with Greek columns—danced and crumbled. A part of her mind was constantly shutting a door on the knowledge that she had to go there that night.

"We called upon the Packs, Mrs. Pigeon, this morning, a most distasteful interview. The man's brood is uncouth. If any of his young grave-robbers come calling here, you are under my instructions to send them——"

Here Great-Uncle Felix swerving from the pun she saw in his

path and savouring it without saying it, took on all the symptoms of a hen with hysterics. His mirth even seemed to reconcile him to the Packs, for when he had mopped everything that had come under the machine-gun spray of soup with his napkin, he confided in Bertie,

"Excellent for the digestion! Laughter is a great releaser of tensions. Even the Packs have their uses!"

The rest of that day was spent in uneasily waiting for the night. Bertie didn't examine her decision to go to the Knowe as she had been bidden, but she knew the decision had been taken, and now all she wanted was to get whatever it was that was going to happen over.

Tea Bertie had, rather cosily, with Mrs. Pigeon and Maudie in the kitchen, as Great-Uncle Felix was having his in his study, because he was "extremely busy with my plans"—Bertie supposed for the Folly. Apprehensive as she was, she could get a certain amount of enjoyment out of watching Maudie solemnly decanting molasses from a huge stone jar into a glass dish for "Mr. Featherstone's tray"—it finally fell from the spoon with the sort of noise people make in films when they go under for the last time in a quagmire. Maudie poured out milk with a sprinkling of wheatgerm powder, while Mrs. Pigeon, without apparently noticing the contrast, busied herself with the forbidden teapot and with setting out a criminal white sliced loaf. Bertie wondered if she oughtn't to disapprove of Mrs. Pigeon for acting so in contradiction of her employer's orders, but Mrs. Pigeon looked so guiltlessly happy drinking her tea that Bertie had to smile at her. Mrs. Pigeon smiled back, warmly.

"There, dear. Help yourself to some jam. I made it myself last summer, and the strawberries were at their very best. There's a chocolate cake to follow, too." She nodded, with the comfortable look of one who knows she is bestowing a treat, and Maudie, who had come back from the study and delivering the tray, stirred her tea in noisy rapture.

"What did you think of Mr. Pack and his children, dear? You mustn't take any notice of Mr. Featherstone, he gets very worked up over things. I daresay none of them meant to be rude to him, I'm sure."

Bertie found that she didn't really know what she thought of them, now she was asked. Her impressions were so involved and overshadowed with what had happened with the elfstone that she didn't even really want to speak about them.

"I don't think they meant to be rude, but Gawain and he didn't see eye to eye over digging up the"—she hesitated at what to call it to Mrs. Pigeon, 'Knowe' seemed somehow affected—"the mound."

"I'm glad Mr. Featherstone doesn't like it. I don't think it's right at all, the idea."

"You mean, digging up graves and things?"

Mrs. Pigeon seemed about to say something and then looked at Maudie and stopped. "Well—perhaps, dear. It is Mr. Featherstone's land, after all."

"Proper cheek, I call it," Maudie was happily spreading strawberry jam like a red eiderdown on her bread. "Anyway, they wouldn't let them get away with it."

"Who wouldn't?" Bertie wondered if she had heard aright.

Maudie's eyes were vague. "Well, they wouldn't, would they?"

"Now then, Maudie," Mrs. Pigeon had begun to push the cups about almost as if she were embarrassed about something, "you don't want to waste too much time. There's all that cleaning the silver to be done before you go, don't forget."

Maudie began to eat hastily, obviously determined that whatever the task, she wasn't going to be done out of her tea. Mrs. Pigeon plied Bertie with chocolate cake, and Bertie, with her mouth full of it, was trying to pick the best words for her next question when Mrs. Pigeon said suddenly,

"You see, dear, it isn't right, meddling with old things like that. People round here say it brings bad luck. I don't know about that, I'm sure they say a lot of silly things, but there's no sense in inviting trouble, is there?"

"You mean, there's a sort of superstition about the place," said Bertie slowly, bunching the crumbs on her plate for another mouthful, and not looking at Mrs. Pigeon.

"That's it exactly, dear." Mrs. Pigeon seemed quite relieved.

"—And you must be careful not to go there at night or they'll get you," burst in Maudie, clogged with chocolate cake, "and you don't come back for a hundred years and then it's too late 'cos everyone you know is dead."

"That's quite enough of that," Mrs. Pigeon's motherly face took on the severest expression Bertie had yet seen on it. "You know you shouldn't go repeating things like that."

"But that's all fairy stories—like Rip Van Winkle. You don't mean people round here still believe in fairy stories in the middle of the twentieth century!" Bertie heard her own voice sounding almost hysterical.

"What people believe in is their own affair. Funny things can happen in the middle of the twentieth century as well as at any time."

"And it does happen to people, 'cos it happened to old Mrs. Fairlee in the village." Maudie didn't seem as daunted by Mrs. Pigeon as she might have been. She nodded her head decidedly. "She came back, they all say she came back."

"What do you mean, 'came back'?"

"Maudie is just repeating idle gossip."

"Well, repeat it to me, Maudie, I want to know." Bertie knew she was being rude, but at the same time there was a strange urgency in her. It was really important that she should know.

"This old Mrs. Fairlee fell asleep one day, like, by the Knowe" (Maudie was evidently familiar with the word) "only she wasn't old then, at all, she was about my age, but it was ages and ages ago——"

"Long before I was born," put in Mrs. Pigeon, who, once the story was started, didn't seem reluctant to contribute to it. "They say it was a hundred years to the day when she turned up again."

"But where had she gone?"

"Oh, nobody knew that. She just disappeared. They all thought she'd run away because she was in trouble in the village."

"*She* said she'd been in there," Maudie's earnest look might at another time have made Bertie want to laugh, but not now. Not when she meant the Knowe. "Only a night, she said she'd been, dancing and that." Maudie's eyes grew wistful. "Lovely spread there was, she said, too, everything she liked best."

"But what did she *look* like, after all that time?"

"Oh, all old and nasty, like an old witch. Of course, they said she was round the bend and took her away."

Mrs. Pigeon piled the plates together dismissively. "It was a very sad story. She died shortly afterwards in a mental home."

"Oh, it was a shock. Seeing her parents' graves and that, when the day before they were alive and well, and hearing that they'd died a long time ago hoping to hear from her right up to the last."

Bertie felt rather sick and wished Maudie wouldn't dwell on it so gloatingly. Of course, it probably was, in fact, some old lady, out of her mind, who had turned up one day in the village with some peculiar story . . . but, somehow, that didn't sound nearly as convincing as what she'd heard.

"They say she said that when she woke up, she didn't know where she was at first, or why she couldn't get up easy. Then she remembered the dancing and thought she was stiff but of course she was just horribly old and couldn't move properly or anything. Just imagine, if I was to wake up tomorrow a hundred years old !"

There was a loud, groaning whirr and a tinny jangling which made Bertie jump, and the sweat break out on her forehead.

"It's all right, dear, just Mr. Featherstone ringing the bell for his tea tray to be taken away. Doesn't like it hanging about in the study in case his papers get sticky—hurry up, Maudie, he knows just how long it should take you to get to the study from here—he did it with a stopwatch, dear," (this to Bertie) "at a sort of little run, with small steps, you know, because of Maudie not having long legs like him, it did look odd, I must say."

Bertie, still shaken both by the bell and what they had been talking about, could just about see her great-uncle mincing seriously from kitchen to study, stopwatch in hand, at the pace he considered right for a deferential jog-trotting female, but she didn't feel up to being amused, any more than you want to laugh in the middle of a nightmare. She had to get out of the kitchen, and go somewhere where she didn't have to talk to anyone, where she could think about what she was going to do—no that was impossible,—where she could do something that would take her mind off what she was going to have to do, that night.

# CHAPTER

# 7

Now she had been there for a bit, it didn't seem so petrifyingly dark. The clouds that had covered the moon when she first got outside had blown away in the light, brisk wind which had got up, and it silvered the chimney tops like twisted barley-sugar, glittered on the rough hair of the Knowe. It looked like a dream, the view from the Knowe in the moonlight of the house beyond, with its gardens and yew hedges drawn up round it like an embroidered coverlet, with the toy trees behind it and the night hills in the distance. A week ago, and it would have been a dream, she wouldn't even have recognised the view. She would certainly have dismissed as a dream what had happened that night already, the creeping downstairs in the dark, terrified of anyone hearing the elderly treads creak in the asthmatic way she had hardly noticed by daylight, terrified of Great-Uncle Felix appearing in his dressing-gown from somewhere, moustache bristling, perhaps shouting at her, terrified, also, of *not* being caught, of having to go on, without any excuse to stay away. For a moment, she thought she had found her excuse, in the great lock and bolts on the outer door, but that was before she remembered what he had said about the elfstone.

She had taken it out of her pocket and, not quite knowing what to do with it, had presented it at the door in a helpless way. As it approached, something happened inside the lock, as though a magnet had gripped it and, with a smooth click, it turned, and at the same moment, above and below, the huge bolts slid obediently back in their sockets. The way was clear. The Opener had opened.

The way to the Knowe, through the yews in the garden cut into shapes that in daylight looked reasonable or at least amusing, was all part of the horrible dream she had been living since that morning. The yews were tall, gardeners had been clipping them for more than a hundred years, they were densely black in the shadows and at night something seemed to live inside their shapes. She had at one moment the idea that the Opener might work on them too, without her wanting it.

The last part of getting to the Knowe, over the field, was almost a relief; though it seemed to come to meet her, growing against the stars as she ran, she was at least coming nearer to getting it over, whatever it was.

Arrived at last, she crouched, panting, by the side of the Knowe. He had said midnight, and her watch in the moonlight told her it was two minutes to twelve. She didn't have to do anything else, it was up to them.

Somewhere, from the village church probably, there began a faint chiming, brought by the breeze that ruffled the hair on the Knowe. Midnight.

She had been holding the elfstone in her hand, in a state of readiness, and her hand was drawn to the Knowe as though it were the other part of a giant magnet. It never touched because there was nothing there, in that moment, to touch. There was a doorway, instead, let into the Knowe, and out of it poured music and light.

Bertie was drawn into the doorway without noticing she was moving, the impulse to seek the source of that music and light was so natural and strong.

The nearest thing she could ever compare it with, afterwards, was to a marvellous party where not knowing anyone there really didn't matter, for once. Some of the light came from torches, but they cast shadows more than anything and she couldn't see the roof. It felt as if it went on up in the dark over her head for a long way. Some of the light seemed to come from the people themselves, who were dancing, or from the cups on the tables.

Someone was playing a harp near her and as his hand struck the wires and drew a ripple of sound from them it seemed to her that she could see the notes escaping and they, too, brought light into the place.

This, then, was the inside of the Knowe, these must be 'they'. Even now she wouldn't put a more definite name to them, was even reluctant to look at them more closely, though nobody appeared to be interested in her. Her impression was more of shimmer and glitter than of people, the dancing involved her in a swirl of skirts and sleeves, all as airy and sparkling as gauze threaded with gold, and scented with the smell of flowers.

Among the faces, beautiful and laughing, turned to her and then turned away again in the dance, there came a face she recognised. He made his way through the dancers to her and it was strange to realise they knew each other; in the throng of the other faces his looked different. It was not full of light, it was pale, earthen-looking, almost like a corpse among the living, and it was not smiling but sad, as she remembered it from that morning, years away. In that place which breathed happiness it came as a shock, like cold water dashed in the face. Bertie felt suddenly sobered, more awake.

"I came." She was proud of that, and anxious for his approval.

"It was laid upon you."

She wasn't even to get the credit for that awful journey. He took her hand again, and the strangeness of that was lost in the strangeness of everything else.

As he led her through the dancers, the scent was that of a summer garden on a warm evening, the spangles of light on their clothes like the sun on waves hurrying joyously to shore. Someone was singing now, the sound seemed to rain down from the roof like the song of a skylark. Bertie longed to join in the dance, to move to that voice, drown in the scent and light, but his hand held hers and guided her on.

They stopped before someone who sat and watched the dancers from a chair with steps up to it and a canopy over it. Bertie had seen pictures of chairs like it in history-books. As her memory informed her, quite uselessly, that it was called a dais, her mind took in the fact that it was a throne. She who was on it leant forward in a sparkle of silver light, and a voice spoke in her head, blending somehow with the light.

"You are welcome here, stranger. We thank you for your coming."

And that's civil enough, thought Bertie, obstinately refusing to think over the rubbish her memory was gabbling about Fairy Queens. This had to be a dream, she wasn't going to let it be anything else. She permitted herself to look at the person on the throne.

Crazily enough, she looked a bit like Mother. Only, even to the loyal Bertie, a good three times as beautiful, a sort of Mother to the power of n. Perhaps a cross between her mother and a beautiful white cat. She was smiling, and leaning down. The scent was overpowering, but it was the scent of primroses and violets that you never smell except very faintly.

"We need a messenger into your world and we have chosen you to be that messenger."

Why me, asked Bertie silently, and the voice in her head explained.

"Because you are of an age to be between worlds. You have been in the world of a child and you are entering that of a grown being of your race. Between worlds there are places out of time, and we do not move in your time. In another year, perhaps another month, we might not have reached you."

Oh great, thought Bertie wildly, just my luck.

The voice in her head purred just like a cat's. "It is indeed your luck. You are fortunate to be chosen, because those who can perform what we ask are rewarded well."

Bertie had by now realised that if you hear voices inside your head it isn't particularly surprising if they know what's going on there. Not surprising, just embarrassing, like having one's mind undressed.

"You wonder why we ask? But you must sit, and drink, and be our guest, before we open that to you. Sit here, near to us."

Bertie, rather awkwardly, sat where the long hand, rainbowed with rings, indicated, on one of the steps to the throne, closer than she wanted to the glittering skirts and that faint but overwhelming scent. A child dressed all in gold appeared before her and offered a gold tray and a gold cup. The light she had noticed before coming from the cups seemed now in fact to come from the liquid in it. She hoped it was white wine, which she much preferred to red. A delicious smell, cool and fruity, made her long to drink it down at one gulp. The voice purred to her to take it.

She was stretching out her hand eagerly for the cup when another hand got in her way and lifted it slowly as though to offer it more ceremoniously. Looking up, she saw his face again, not so much sad this time as intent, the eyes dark and wide, fixed on her. Something played back in her memory, but the skirts behind her stirred quickly and the memory blurred.

"Drink, and seal our friendship."

Surely the purring voice now sounded just a little like Mother's coaxing her to take some medicine? Her hand drew back—*take nothing that they offer or you will regret it,* wasn't that the last thing he had said this morning?—and now she read the warning again in his eyes.

"Would you rather eat before you drink?"

There was a gold plate, she was too confused to see where it had come from, but now she was determined to shut her nostrils against it whatever it was. No doubt they knew better than she did at the moment what her favourite food was. She remembered the "spread" Maudie had gloated over, and poor Mrs. Fairlee had enjoyed.

She shook her head, mutely, at the offered plate. Somehow, ideas about being polite and thanking people didn't obtain in circumstances like these, when you thought what they were really doing.

She felt the anger coming from behind her just as she would feel a wind upon her cheek, but she was more frightened of what might happen if she drank than she was of offending, so she just set herself tight inside and waited.

"You do not know what you miss, friend, or you would take our hospitality. There is life in it of a sort you cannot guess at, which people would sell their souls to taste."

Well. I'm hanging on to mine, thought Bertie, and felt a

tremor in her mind as though the cat had smiled and decided to relax.

"We will not press you, then. We would have wished to have you as a friend and companion for this night" (*not if it's a hundred years long, thank you*). "But that is not what matters now. We need your help—oh yes, we cannot manipulate your world just as we please, there are laws that govern all things, ourselves as well. There are barriers, of time and place, which it would not serve you to know" (*but it's lucky I know about poor old Mrs. Fairlee, all the same*) "but there are points where our worlds overlap. This," and Bertie felt the hand behind her make a circling gesture, and the primroses breathed strongly on her, "is one of them. You can see it as part of your Reality. To you it is a pile of earth and grass, to us our feasting place and home. Formerly men knew this, and respected it. In days not long gone by—but yesterday in our reckoning—no man would have come near. Now," she paused, and Bertie waited without turning round. She would sooner not look at that beautiful face with its frightening deception of familiarity. "Now, they have forgotten and they see only the surface of things. They would do that which we must resist, with all our power."

Bertie suddenly realised that the dancing had stopped, and the dancers were all around them, in a silent, shining circle. She could hear the faint splutter of the torches and felt the listening darkness in the great roof of the Knowe.

"They would break open the Knowe itself."

There was a rustle from the circle and it pressed closer. Bertie felt dizzy, as though she were holding her breath and it was suffocating her. Her mind searched wildly for reasons. Why should anybody do it? I don't understand—her thoughts trailed away. Of course she understood. What about the Packs, and their wanting Great-Uncle Felix to let them excavate the Knowe? But, after all, what did they think the Knowe was? *Wasn't* it a burial mound—and, if it was, how could it be this too?

There was a motion of impatience behind her.

"Why cannot it be so? The minds of mortals move as clumsily as their bodies. Is not your earth many things to you? You till it for life, and in death you cover your bodies with it. If those

57

you think of were ω come here, in our Place, they would find what they expect to find, bones and necklaces and human trash— but they would destroy what they know nothing of."

*I don't see what I can do.*

"You must not let this happen. Speak with those who would do it."

*But they wouldn't believe me!*

"You need not speak of what you have seen and heard here. Their hearts and eyes are shut to us, but not to you. Use what human wit you have to help you."

*Supposing I can't manage?*

"We have not yet lost all our powers."

There was a murmur like that of angry bees all round, and Bertie's skin prickled.

"You already know of one whom our lives have touched." Bertie was reminded of a spinning top colliding with something and jerkily breaking its rhythm and collapsing. "And those who interfere we have our own ways of punishing. You should read and listen," there was irony in the cat's voice, no purr now, "to know what they are."

Bertie put her head into her hands, with the vague idea of hiding from that relentless glitter, from the dangerous hum all round her, from the cold, soft voice in her head.

"We shall send our servant to you again, and you shall show us that you mean to do our commands. Now return to your world."

A hand pressed on Bertie's head so that, still held in her hands, it was forced forward on to her knees; and with the pressure came overwhelming drowsiness, her lids dropped with her head and a tide of sleep rolled over her.

# CHAPTER

## 8

It was cold, piercingly cold. Bertie moved uneasily, close to waking but not awake. In her sleep she told herself that she had better not dream any more conversation, because the inverted commas would let in the cold air. A few minutes later, she was awake and smiling at her logic.

Then it was no time to smile. The grass under her was wet with the night dew, the wind sang in her ears, everything came back like an ugly dream that leaves its taste in the brain.

First things first, Bertie scolded herself, trying to rub some life into her arms and legs. You must get back to bed before anyone finds you've been gone—and what would Mother think of your sleeping out on the grass at night? She shook her head quickly as the memory of Mother's dear face got muddled with the memory of another, so lately seen—or was it?

She could not really doubt anything, not out there, in the convincing chill before dawn, with the Knowe's black shape reminding at her side. What else could have got her out there? A very energetic bout of sleepwalking, she supposed, but it had certainly been combined with a very odd set of hallucinations.

Was her mind giving way under strain? Perhaps that was what it all meant. After Daddy's accident and everything, it wasn't so unlikely. And hadn't Granny gone mad? There was something Mother had hinted at, and Daddy never spoke about his mother—that sort of thing was supposed to be hereditary, too.

Bertie leant her head against the Knowe in the cold wind and shivered with terror.

The fear seemed to roll over her like the tide of sleep earlier, and, like that too, it receded after a bit. Bertie even drew some comfort from the rough hide of the Knowe. Come to think of it, there was an awful lot of sense, in a funny kind of way, in her madness.

It hung together, what she thought she had heard that night, even down to the falling asleep, like old Mrs. Fairlee.

Like old Mrs. Fairlee! Fresh terror broke over Bertie. She felt her cold stiff arms and legs, peered at them in the dim light, half expecting to touch the swollen joints of old age, to feel the flaccid wrinkles drooping her cheeks, but a second was enough to reassure her that she hadn't slept away a hundred years, and it was the same body she had come out in, so to speak.

The fear had woken her properly, though, out of her daze of cold and confusion, and her first urgency returned. Get home, get to bed, get warm, then sort it out, was the right programme, and she got up and began to run, clumsily because of cold and stiffness, towards the twisted silhouette of the house against the clouds. It didn't seem possible that there were people asleep in there, Mrs. Pigeon with chintzy curtains drawn against the grey light Bertie was running in, Great-Uncle Felix she could see in some Disney fantasy sucking in the hairs on his moustache and whistling them out again in some wall-rattling snore—both without the least idea what she had been through, even without the least idea that she was outside. Not that they would believe if they knew—but then: Bertie, stumbling as she ran, wondered about Mrs. Pigeon. She had joined in quite heartily when Maudie had got going. All she had really been reluctant about was letting Bertie hear the story about Mrs. Fairlee in the first place.

Unfortunately, it wasn't Mrs. Pigeon she had to convince. Before she could start thinking about the impossible task she had been set, she had reached the bit of garden before the house, with the clipped yew shapes that had watched her pass between them to the Knowe. In the dawn light they were less frightening, something of their vitality had ebbed with the coming of the day. She got through them quite quickly and found herself in front of the huge oak door. As she put her hand up to swing the door open into the refuge of the house, she could think only of the bed that was waiting for her, of warm blankets and forgetful sleep.

Several times on the stairs she was sure the noise she was making would wake someone up. The house itself seemed to be protesting at her return as though she was alien to its atmosphere. Suddenly, she prinked both little fingers and minced up the next stair, mouthing, with a simper, "No wonder! I've been in Fairyland." She held on to the newel post, giggling weakly. *Oh shut up, if you think that you'll go bonkers. Perhaps you've gone bonkers and that's why you're thinking it.* Desperately, the joke suddenly very sour, Bertie gained her bedroom, opened the door, which groaned spitefully at her, and, dragging her clothes off anyhow, scuffled into bed. The light through the windows was brighter now, gave a silver edge to the curtains and the dressing-table mirror, made it easy to shut one's eyes against it, easy to see another silver light with a cat's voice in it, easy to fall into the spinning, dark cavern beyond the voice, deep down past hearing and sight.

"Wake up, dear! Wake up—what a sound sleeper you are, you must have been tired out yesterday—wake *up*, dear, are you all right?"

Mrs. Pigeon's anxious face suspended over hers did not make Bertie feel any less sick with sleep, she just wanted to flap her hand feebly at her, as though she were a fly buzzing round her face, and get her to go away. Though she didn't look like a fly, really, more like a hedgehog with stomach ache. The desire to grin at this brought Bertie a little more awake.

"You really must get up, dear, Mr. Featherstone doesn't like anyone to be late for breakfast, he's never late himself."

"Doesn't he ever feel terrible and not want to get up?" Bertie bicycled the blankets off, letting the cool air on her legs rouse her a little. Mrs. Pigeon was fussing about, picking up her clothes from the floor.

"You shouldn't treat your nice things like this, dear, I could have trodden on them coming in——"

"It looks like a sort of paper chase leading to the bed. The underwear trail." Bertie rubbed her eyes tenderly, they felt as if she had hot sand in them. "But doesn't he ever get ill?"

Mrs. Pigeon raised a flushed face from rescuing tights under the valance of the bed. "Never since I've known him. Mr. Featherstone prides himself on keeping his health by living sensibly, as you know, dear, which reminds me, I haven't made the muesli for your breakfast yet, and he won't let me buy the packaged stuff, I must rush off, it takes so long to chop those nuts, now you will be sure to hurry, dear, won't you?"

Bertie, left alone, toyed with the idea of getting back into bed and pretending she was ill—she certainly wasn't all *right*—but Mrs. Pigeon would probably get the worst of that, and Great-Uncle Felix might come up and start unloading some super-abominable herbal remedies, "take a little tincture of tossifrage, swallow a live mouse dipped in molasses, and you'll be as right as rain, either that, or you'll feel like a proper shower".

It was no good, sooner or later she'd have to face up to it, she had to get up, she had to go down and get breakfast, she had to think about what had happened, she even had to do something about it. That was ridiculous and impossible, granted, but what was the alternative? She didn't know, except that they had powers to harm which they would use. What had *she* said about reading and listening? She'd picked up something about what *not* to do by listening to Maudie—and wouldn't she be surprised to know how useful she'd been;—and to *him*, she didn't know what to call him, the messenger, perhaps. She put cold water out of the flowered china jug on her eyes, and, with them still shut, began to brush her hair furiously. Of course, she got in a bash on the side of the head from the wrong side of the brush, first go, just the thing to put the thoughts in order.

*Why* had he given that warning about not eating or drinking? After all, he was one of them, wasn't he? She remembered how different he had looked, with his face pale like that of an ill man, among theirs. But if he didn't belong, what was he doing there?

A gong went down in the hall, with a kind of frightened clamour, like a bird beating its wings, Mrs. Pigeon sending up a last distress signal. Bertie slung her belt round her hastily, buckled it and ran out.

Great-Uncle Felix greeted her arrival in the dining-room rather coldly, perhaps she was meant to be on her marks outside, waiting for the first stroke of the gong to hare in? As she raised her spoon to dip it into the rather crowded bowl before her—moosley, had Mrs. Pigeon called it?—he removed the bowl to peer at it attentively. With her frustrated spoon hovering in the air, she felt like someone out of a Chaplin film.

"Ah, the proportion of sultanas is somewhat low, Mrs. Pigeon. You may be sure the Arabs have a good reason for prizing dried fruits, Roberta, they contain the very essence of nourishment. They enable one to cross the desert without losing too many valuable vitamins." He replaced the bowl, and waved his hand airily. "Continue, continue."

I haven't *begun*, thought Bertie resentfully, stirring up what looked like a mess of cereal and apples and raisins and nuts, and who's going to cross a desert anyway? She felt cross, and dazed with lack of sleep, and unable even to think about her problems.

"There's a letter for you, dear. Under your napkin."

Bertie dropped her spoon and scuffled under the napkin, sending it unheeded to the floor. A letter! That could only mean Mother, nobody else knew she was there, so there would be news about Daddy and whether he was getting better all right—and whether he and Mother were going to stay together.

It was Mother's handwriting. Her fingers became suddenly so clumsy that she could hardly tear the envelope open.

"Use a knife, Roberta, use a knife."

It was jaggedly open at last, and she had got the closely written letter out and unfolded. She had no wish to read it under the gaze of Mrs. Pigeon and Great-Uncle Felix, who was masticating rhythmically but quite alive to everything that was going on.

"From your mother, Roberta? I trust your father is surviving the attentions of my sister. You have my permission to read at breakfast."

"Thank you so much," It was difficult to sound properly ironic to a man who continued to revolve his moustache in two-four time, and who didn't seem to notice you were being ironic. Anyway, she had to read it now.

Mother wrote in her usual practical but hurried way; she never used full stops but put dashes between sentences which made everything seem rather excited and dramatic. Daddy was picking up strength, she wasn't to worry about him, the doctor said he was getting over the concussion slowly but he would be all right in the end. He fretted rather, which made it difficult, as of course Granny did, too, and they made each other worse. Bertie could just see it, Daddy was always a little faddy about his health, and Granny loved to fuss, especially over him, and, now, after the accident—she was sorry for poor Mother between the two of them. If only she doesn't get too sick of them . . . the cold, dull feeling of fear was again in Bertie's stomach as she read. After all, Mother was making a big effort, this was Daddy's chance to put everything all right again—if it fell through . . .

"Roberta, I was speaking to you. How is your father?"

"Oh, he's much better, thank you."

"I hope his appetite is returning. It is useless to expect convalescence to progress if there is no appetite."

Bertie looked at her letter helplessly. The words were already beginning to rainbow and swim. Whatever happened, she mustn't burst out crying *again* in front of them.

"I expect it all has to take time, Mr. Featherstone. After an accident like that, you wouldn't really fancy anything for quite a bit, would you? Do you remember how Moss was off his food for a long time after he fell off that ladder last summer? He used to come into the kitchen and watch me getting a meal and say it fair made his stomach turn."

"I remember perfectly." Great-Uncle Felix was bristling with the memory, and Bertie, blinking to clear her eyes, was dumbly grateful to Mrs. Pigeon. "He refused my offer of a diet sheet quite insolently, quite insolently. If gardeners were not so difficult to get, I should have felt myself justified in giving him notice. As it was, I declined to interest myself in his recovery."

*Bully for him.* And I bet he got well in record time, thought Bertie, spooning in the muesli. At least Daddy wasn't here. He'd never have got better and Mother would have gone round the bend. She said in her letter that she hoped Bertie wasn't finding things too impossible, "the house is lovely, though, and you mustn't forget to have a look at the Knowe. I used to find it

64

fascinating, though nobody could tell me much about it, just a lot of superstition."

"I hope you are not intending to go anywhere this morning, Roberta."

Bertie had wistful visions of going down to the station—it would be quite a trudge, actually—buying a ticket to Sherborne and surprising Mother. The trouble was, it wouldn't be just a surprise, but a nuisance as well.

"No. There isn't anywhere to go, is there?"

Luckily Great-Uncle Felix was short on irony-detection that morning, but she could see Mrs. Pigeon fidgetting nervously with her wholemeal toast. Well, you couldn't dismiss nieces any more than you could gardeners, they were in even shorter supply.

"I ask," continued Great-Uncle Felix indistinctly through the napkin with which he was massaging his mouth, "because that fellow Pack rang before breakfast, I had entirely forgotten that I had invited him to examine the plans for my Folly. It seems he thought I included his ill-mannered brood in his invitation, so I shall require you, Roberta, to entertain them while I show Pack the plans. I will not expose my ideas to that uncouth young vandal and his barbarian sister. You will have to remove them from my sight." He rose grandly, forced his napkin through the ornate silver ring, and stalked from the room. Mrs. Pigeon helped herself quickly to some more butter, and spread it lavishly on her toast.

"How *can* I entertain them—they're absolutely ghastly, so stuck-up and know-all—this just about ruins the whole day——"

"I'm sorry for them, dear, myself, no mother, at least, she's not much use to them married to someone else, is she?—and brought up by that Mr. Pack, I don't think he knows what they're doing half the time, or cares, while he's poking about with that archaeology of his, no better than messing about with mud, I call it, science though it may be. Those two young things'd be better off with a father who cared more about them and less about digging up bones."

Bertie put aside a vision of Mr. Pack, with impassive face to the ground, scrabbling hard and sending out showers of earth backward between his knees, and considered. This angle on the super-

65

cilious Packs was a new one to her. Thinking of them as neglected and pathetic—though the memory of Gawain's eyebrows and Clothilde looking over her spectacles didn't really fit either adjective—made her feel less at a disadvantage in the coming encounter. She would have to remember hard about their mother when they were actually there.

# CHAPTER

9

"How's the book getting on?"

"The book?"

"The one you're writing on the house. Or have you finished it and started another?"

Why had she ever laid claim to anything so idiotic in the first place? It was particularly irritating as she was sure Gawain didn't believe she was writing a book at all, but she was forced to keep up the pretence because she didn't know how to drop it without making herself seem even more of an idiot. No doubt there was a way of shrugging it all off with some witty remark, but as she couldn't think of the remark that was that.

"Of course these things take a lot of time. You have to do plenty of research—and verify it." She was pleased with "verify".

Clothilde, propped on her shoulders on the brick wall, her hips on the worn wooden bench and legs straight out in front of her—her trousers were just the shade of purple Bertie hadn't been able to get the last time she was in London—spat out the piece of grass between her teeth. "I suppose by book you mean project. I'm surprised you bother to do your holiday tasks at all, we just put in a morning on it before we go back—they never know how long you've taken, after all, and it's stupid to waste holiday time."

Naturally I'm stupid and you're clever, thought Bertie, and, aloud, with a wave of the hand that she realised as she was making it came straight from Great-Uncle Felix, "Oh no, I wouldn't bother with a project. This is going to be a proper book."

"Have you chosen your publisher yet?" Gawain's voice was perfectly polite, but Clothilde started to laugh, which in her position was to invite suffocation, so she sat up abruptly, rocking the bench and preventing Bertie's reply.

"Let's do something, for heaven's sake, if we've got to be here. How about your showing us the house, then? Good practice for writing it down, you can tell us first. We might even tip you at the end if you do it properly."

Bertie didn't say anything for a minute because she couldn't think of anything to say. She didn't know a rotten thing about the house, she hadn't even been over it all, and certainly nobody had told her anything about it, so she had nothing whatever to go on. Could she invent the whole thing from scratch? Perhaps to somebody else, if she were in the right mood, but surely not under the sardonic gaze of these two.

"As far as I'm concerned, you needn't bother with the house, *that*," Gawain pointed a long arm towards the hump of the Knowe brooding in the distance, "is what I want to see. Father's creaking to see it, too, but he daren't dash up to it in full sight or your uncle'll go even further round the twist than he is already. So if you lead on, at least I can tell him about it."

"There's nothing to tell." Bertie felt defensive and frightened. Better the house than this. *She* knew how dangerous the Knowe was. They didn't want strangers messing about there—particularly strangers who wanted to break the Knowe open.

She put a hand over her mouth. How could she have forgotten, till that minute, what she was supposed to be doing! The whole point was to put them clean off any idea of digging it up, or something ghastly would happen. What form it would take she hadn't the faintest idea, but she didn't doubt it could happen and would obviously concern her, be ghastly for her personally. What was the most frightful thing, at the moment, that could go wrong?

"You having another of your turns?" Clothilde was surveying her critically. "You know, you ought to see a doctor rather than muck about with these health cures. You look awful. Doesn't she?"

68

Gawain's eyes, perhaps because he didn't wear spectacles, didn't seem as critical. "She looks tired, one readily admits, a bit wan under the eye-sockets, but not actually ready for the plague-pit yet. Probably sitting up too late over her research. What you need is a brisk walk—in that direction. Lead on, MacBerta."

"There's nothing to show. Honestly. I don't know why you're interested."

"Then we'll tell you quietly, in words of five syllables, while we walk together. I don't know what they teach them nowadays, but it isn't respect for archaeology. Heavy tutting."

This was the signal for Clothilde to start laughing again. I'm glad somebody finds him funny, thought Bertie crossly, finding herself having to run to catch up with them as they set out for the Knowe. I'll just have to hope they find it terribly dreary, because I don't know the first thing about how to put them off it from an archaeology point of view. She matched her stride to Gawain's.

"What makes you think it's worth digging up, anyway?"

"The reply to that is what the man said about climbing the mountain. Because it's there."

"But it's silly to go digging up things that might be a waste of effort."

"They mightn't, and that's the point. Think how nice for Father to turn up some Bronze Age finds thousands of years old. Can't you see how romantic?"

"It would be someone's grave, wouldn't it?"

"Not much point if it wasn't. That size, it would be a chieftain's. Mass burial, you know, all the loved ones half-nelsoned into the grave after you. Make you keep watching after his health while he was alive, all right."

"Don't you think it's rather horrible, disturbing somebody's bones like that?"

It was Clothilde who paused, her hand on the white wicket gate that shut off the garden of the clipped yews from the field.

"For heaven's sake, why? They're dead, aren't they?"

"But they took all that trouble over burying themselves properly—they couldn't possibly have thought of anyone having so little—reverence" (Bertie hurried on, ignoring Clothilde's raised eyebrows and patient expression) "as to root them up and mess them about like that. I mean, supposing it was your grandmother?"

"My grandmother is alive and well and living in Hampstead, thank you. And if and when she poops, you can bet your last decimal she'd be proud and honoured to be dug up and put in a museum as relics of Twentieth Century Aged Relative."

Clothilde was doing her sick hen stunt again. "Mind you, Ga, I think she'd insist on a rest-period first. What about her favourite speech on the rush and hurry of modern life?"

"O.K. We could declare her a neutral zone for a year, she could put it in her will." Gawain seemed quite pleased with the idea Bertie had originally intended as a wounding reminder of their callousness. "One thing that would have to go with her would be Fairy, if she died first."

"Fairy?"

"The Peke to end all Pekes. Brave as a lion and all that, and smells like a dustbin. We ought to do the thing properly, and get Miss Larkin—she's her maid—to commit suicide, very decently, of course, a lavender-scented cyanide pill, I think, and be buried with her."

Bertie didn't think she was going to get very far appealing to their better feelings. She trudged across the field beside them in silence while Gawain elaborated the list of the friends and helpers of his grandmother who might have a courteous desire to be buried with her. Listening to him, and picking her way over the tufts of hummocky grass, Bertie found it impossible to believe she had covered the same ground, coming back from the Knowe, before dawn that very morning.

"You know, it's quite a compelling object, isn't it? Marching towards us like that." (He noticed it too.) "No wonder people are interested in it."

"People are terrified of it, you mean," Clothilde pressed her glasses up on her nose and looked severely at the Knowe. "I bet round here they give it a wide berth. Don't they?"

"I don't know. I've only been here a couple of days. Why should they?" Bertie's heart was pounding.

"Have you forgotten what I told you about the Neolithic

arrowheads being called elfstones?" (No, teacher, not much fear of that.) "It's the same thing, of course. You'd be amazed the amount of superstition that lingers on in these country districts. This," she gave a familiar pat to the Knowe as they reached it, "is supposed to be the place the fairies dance in. Haven't you read any fairy stories? All about the door that opens in the side of it, and the unwary traveller going in, and before he knows where he is, he's eaten and drunk fairy food and he's stuck there for as long as they want him."

Gawain placed his back against the Knowe and slithered down till he was in a comfortable heap at the bottom. His examination of the Knowe on his father's behalf evidently wasn't going to lead to anything too strenuous.

"Puzzle being, why should they want him?" He selected a piece of grass, broke it and stuck it rakishly in his mouth. "From all accounts, they're twice as pretty as we are."

"Perhaps to remind them?" Bertie found herself feverishly interested in the conversation. Hadn't she been told to find out more by listening? "They could look at him and think they're twice as nice." (Makes them sound like a lot of supercilious Packs. But they weren't like that, they weren't like that at all.)

"It's never said what exactly they want them for, so perhaps they don't even want them. Perhaps the victims get sucked in——"

"Into a kind of vortex," Bertie supplied eagerly. Had she deliberately walked into the Knowe last night? She only remembered being inside suddenly.

"Mm. Sort of drain. It's an idea." Gawain took out his piece of grass, and gravely selected a fresh bit. "Clothilde's the folk-lore expert. What do you think?"

Clothilde seemed pleased at this appeal. She, too, arranged grass in her mouth, and thought. Bertie sat beside them, her back also against the warm side of the Knowe, and gazed with them at the twisted chimneys of Longbarrow. It would have been peaceful, she thought with despair, if only she could forget what had happened, or, simply, disbelieve it.

"One of the ballads says the Fairy Queen takes a fancy to a young man and is a bit sick when his girl rescues him."

"How did the Queen get him in the first place?"

"He tells the girl a cold wind blew him off his horse. Some wind. Anyway, however he'd got mixed up in it all, he didn't start, like some, by walking into one of these." She gestured backwards with her thumb. "Then he found himself stuck with these creatures—call them Fairies if you like—and unable to escape. Being in their power didn't stop him running about the countryside, though, and getting up to no good with this girl. So she had a baby coming and her family furious with her, everyone furious with her for letting down the side, her father was a knight and all that, so she had a jolly good reason for rescuing him. He had a jolly good reason for wanting to be rescued too, there's a mysterious bit where he explains the Queen pays a sort of forfeit—it's called a 'teind' in the original," Clothilde's voice became self-consciously learned, "every seven years to hell."

"To *hell*?"

"Yup. Sort of rent? I don't know. Anyway——"

"But . . . I don't understand! What *is* hell?"

"My dear child," Gawain drew up his long legs and sank his chin on his knees, "better girls than you have asked that question. And got no satisfactory answer. Leave out the philosophy, let's take it hell is hell, and let my sister get on with the plot."

"But I don't see how you can have hell *and* Fairyland."

"I don't see why they should be mutually exclusive. According to the stories, human beings can get into both."

Bertie found herself unable to explain that fairy stories were about magic, not morality. Being good or bad, surely, was what people, or some people, thought got you into heaven or hell. What had that got to do with being sucked into Fairyland? It just wasn't the same world.

"Get on with the ballad bit, will you? She promised to listen."

"Well, this young man—he was a knight too of course, ballads are nothing if not class-conscious—somehow knows, or has been told that he's the one they're going to hand over for this teind thing when it falls due, so he'll land up in hell."

"I suppose the fairies didn't fancy giving up one of their own. He must have been an absolute gift to them."

"I thought nobody was going to interrupt?"

"No. I just said *she* wasn't going to interrupt. Carry on."

"Work it out for yourself, then."

Bertie wasn't sure whether Clothilde was really annoyed with Gawain or not, but she certainly didn't look as though she were going on with the story. Gawain, still with his chin on his knees, glanced sideways at her.

"Do-it-yourself folk-lore? Right. He says to the girl, 'You got to get me out of this place fast, see, or I'm for the deep fry.' She says, 'Any suggestions?' and *he* says, 'Come to the Knowe and grab me some night they're busy dancing——' "

"Wrong."

"Wrong. He says, 'I'll be at a certain place at a certain time, and you grab me; hang on, because there'll be a nasty mix-up——' "

"You've read it." Clothilde sounded cross.

"Probably. But it isn't too difficult. There are only a certain number of alternatives, after all, in stories about fairies. She might have had to perform some task or other, I suppose, plenty of those going, tame a wild bull, fetch three hairs from a tiger's nostril—and got the young man as a sort of reward."

The piece of grass between Bertie's fingers snapped suddenly. Perhaps all this was really intended for her. Gawain and Clothilde thought they were talking about something that wasn't real, but then she would have thought that herself, yesterday, before she came to this place. There were things they didn't know about that were real. In what sense they were real she didn't understand, but they were real enough to affect the world she lived in.

Gawain had slithered down, turned over to lie on his stomach, and was prodding the Knowe with one finger.

"Knock, knock. Open sesame. I expect we're just not pretty enough. You haven't noticed any personable young men hanging around here, have you?"

Bertie stared at him quite unable to answer. All kinds of ideas were whirling around in her head, and Gawain himself seemed quite far away. That could easily be the reason why *he* had looked different among the dancers, he was a human being like herself. Hadn't he said something about her not being a prisoner, in a way which implied *he* was? And why had he bothered to give her a warning? They had chosen him as their messenger because he could get through to her, but they couldn't have thought about the possibility of his taking pity on her. Perhaps that wasn't the sort of thing they knew about.

"Hallo, she's off on one of her turns again. You really ought to go to a trick-cyclist and get him to wheel you back to sanity."

"Perhaps it's epilepsy." Clothilde had decided to join them again.

"Wouldn't she be rolling about, biting the grass? I give it to you, she has been biting the grass, but no rolls as yet."

"Don't be silly, that's *grand mal*. She could easily have *petit mal*. It only lasts a second or two sometimes, an electric short-circuit in the brain. Some people don't even know they've got it."

"Maybe everyone has it, and we're all Little Baddies."

This set Clothilde off again, but Bertie looked at them both with irritation. If only she could tell them what kind of a place they were sprawling and giggling against, they'd get up in a hurry—no, they'd fall about even more, because they wouldn't believe her. By the time she'd finished telling them, even Clothilde would be more inclined to the insanity than to the epilepsy theory. But she must, she must, stick to the point, because the really incredible thing was that she kept forgetting it.

"Do you think your father will try and dig this place up?"

"Try, you bet. Whether he'll make it or not all depends on your uncle."

"My great-uncle."

"Your, correction, grandiose uncle. If he sticks his hoofs in, Father can write a nasty article about it, I suppose, but I don't think anyone can *make* a man throw open his grounds to trespassing archaeologists."

Bertie clasped her hands suddenly. She was wasting her time with them. It was Great-Uncle Felix she should be persuading.

# CHAPTER

## 10

"Is your great-uncle going to feed us at any point? It's nearly four and I'm ravenous. This grass is all very well, quietly sustaining in its own way, no doubt, but not really nourishing. I could go for some scones and home-made jam, followed by chocolate cake, any time you care to bring it on."

"You're not likely to get that, anyway. Chocolate is poison and so is white bread. I'm not sure about the jam, but you could always have molasses." Bertie got to her feet, dusting down her jeans. She was quite as anxious as they might be to get back to the house, the sooner she got to grips with this problem of influencing her great-uncle the sooner she could try to forget what might happen. Whatever it was.

"Molasses? I thought that was what Negro slaves used to live on. He goes in for this sort of thing seriously, doesn't he?"

Clothilde joined them, working her toes into a firmer grip of her thonged sandals. "He's not such a bad advertisement, all the same. He looks as spry as an old grasshopper, and I bet he can walk further and faster than Father who slumps in his study all day when he isn't on a dig."

"Well, get ready to place your bets. Here they come. Featherstone rounding the corner by the garden gate now, he's coming into the straight, he's head and head with Pack, they're both showing excellent form, Featherstone leading by perhaps a neck——"

They were walking rather fast, Bertie thought, almost as though they could hear Gawain's commentary. But where was the winning post? It seemed from their direction to be the Knowe. Of course, Great-Uncle Felix wanted to be able to explain to Mr. Pack on the spot his plans for the Folly. Bertie took a deep breath and clenched her fists. Here, if anywhere, was going to be her chance to say something to stop the excavation of the Knowe, but what she was going to say she hadn't the faintest idea. She found she had stood still while the other two were strolling on to meet their father and Great-Uncle Felix, and she had to run to catch up.

"Having a tiny fit back there? I don't know what the health cure is for epilepsy, we'll have to ask Mr. Featherstone. Hallo there, we were just saying, Mr. Featherstone, we'll have to ask you how you're dealing with your great-niece's epilepsy."

Gawain's air of courteous inquiry did nothing to appease Great-Uncle Felix. He had been viewing Bertie's companions, she could see, even at a distance, with some distaste, but this was now turned into open irritation.

"Absurd. Absurd. It is hardly decent to crack feeble jokes on such subjects. Were she suffering from epilepsy I would have been the first to be informed."

Bertie knew perfectly well that the blank faces of Gawain and Clothilde covered an intense desire to laugh, because her own did, too. She also saw the logic of it; if an epileptic niece were coming to stay with him, of course her mother would let him know so he could cope; but this didn't make his statement less ferociously pompous. Mr. Pack had somehow insinuated his bulky shoulders between his children and her great-uncle, and was waving his hand at the Knowe.

"Of course, I can see how the place tempts you—it's really a very commanding position."

"You think so, you think so?" Great-Uncle Felix turned from glaring at Gawain to surveying the Knowe with a softened expression. "It has an excellent view of the house. My Folly could hardly be missed from quite a long way away."

There was a stifled grunt from Gawain, and Bertie was fairly sure Clothilde had pinched him. Mr. Pack weighed in hastily,

"This place is already famous in the neighbourhood, I understand."

"Famous? In what sense?"

"Oh, I would say as an unusual object——"

"Everybody knows the Knowe." Gawain, in spite of a quick frown from his father, raised his hands above his head, and, clicking his fingers, revolved slowly on his heels. Great-Uncle Felix held his face averted, as from a bad smell.

"——and, naturally, it could become much more than an object of interest locally."

A modest smile appeared under Great-Uncle Felix's moustache. "Yes, I expect it could well appear in journals interested in such things. It is entirely my own design, though influenced, I admit, by Inigo Jones. I imagine any architect who takes his business seriously will want to see it. It may be necessary to arrange special visits. I cannot have my work interrupted at all hours."

Mr. Pack did not look very satisfied with this fantasy of pilgrim architects queueing up to disturb his host's peace, but it was also clear to Bertie that he didn't want to make his meaning any plainer under the ironic eye of his son. He smiled vaguely, instead, and began to walk round the Knowe, slapping its sides as though it were a restive horse.

"Very, very interesting. You know, you're lucky to have such a rare example of a Bronze Age barrow on your land, Featherstone. People don't often understand the importance of a thing like this, they put it under the plough, even, level it down to tidy things up, you wouldn't believe what uneducated people are capable of."

"Education isn't always the criterion of sensible behaviour, I'm afraid." Great-Uncle Felix underlined this one with another glare at Gawain, whom Bertie had gradually come to recognise as her greatest ally in the anti-excavation campaign. Doubtless he felt to propitiate Great-Uncle Felix in any way was unworthy of him, no matter what the cause, or perhaps it was sheer contrariness. Probably he just couldn't help being like that to Great-Uncle Felix, there were people you had to behave to in a certain way, they drew certain sorts of behaviour out of you like magnets. It

77

was probably Great-Uncle Felix's moustache setting up a sort of chemical reaction in Gawain.

"Well, we really ought to be getting back, Featherstone. It's been fascinating hearing about your plans like this. If you'll let me, I'd like to drop by some time and tell you something about what *this*," he gave the Knowe a dismissive slap, "is like underneath."

"Delighted, my dear fellow."

Bertie thought, as they all turned to cross the field to the house again, that Great-Uncle Felix sounded polite but not at all enthusiastic. He wasn't the kind of man who enjoyed being told anything. She felt suddenly excited. What did it mean? It meant that Mr. Pack was losing, that Great-Uncle Felix thought the whole excavation idea was a bore, that the Knowe was going to be safe.

But he was going to build his Folly on it.

# CHAPTER
 11

When they got back to the house they found Mrs. Pigeon had got tea ready, but by that time it was too late, as the Packs had been seen into their car in the drive already. Bertie was thankful, for she saw Mrs. Pigeon's ideas of hospitality had partly conquered her fear of Great-Uncle Felix to the extent of a cake with chocolate icing and the immoral appearance of the teapot itself, and the thought of Gawain drinking tea and eating cake in the same room as Great-Uncle Felix was unnerving. There might have been an explosion. As it was, the forecast was threatening.

"What is the meaning of this—this rubbish?"

Mrs. Pigeon's hands went waveringly to her bun, which had started, as usual under stress, to slip its moorings.

"Well, they're used to a proper tea, Mr. Featherstone——"

"A proper tea! Kindly clear away this refuse and bring me what I would designate as a proper tea in my study. And when you have eaten what is on your diet-sheet for this meal, Roberta, I expect to see you there. I have several matters which it is necessary to discuss with you."

This was depressing. Discussing things, whatever they were, in other people's studies never seemed the most attractive timetable in the world; but she was curiously cheered to get an unmistakable wink from Mrs. Pigeon as she caught her hair on its first uncoil and prolonged it with a couple of her ineffectual pins.

"We'll have ours in the kitchen, dear, I think, and Maudie can get Mr. Featherstone's tray for him."

Bertie picked up the cake and the teapot, reassured that neither would be put away in the kitchen till they had been used. She left Mrs. Pigeon loading a tray with the clean plates and knives, and made her way through the baize door, enjoying the way it sighed to after her. It would be nice to have time to explore the house properly, nice to relax and not have things on her mind.

"Oh, isn't that a shame! Wouldn't he let them have it, then? I do think that's awful, I really do."

Bertie couldn't help laughing at Maudie's picture of her Great-Uncle Felix ordering away the tea and cake—she saw it herself as a Victorian picture-that-tells-a-story, with the Packs in various attitudes at the table, Mr. Pack with his head sullenly sunk on his chest, Clothilde smiting her brow in frustration, Gawain with one clawing hand extended to the teapot, a baffled sneer on his face, and, dominating the scene, the tall figure of Great-Uncle Felix, arm and forefinger pointed commandingly at a weeping Mrs. Pigeon, her hair in total surrender on her shoulders, bearing away the two offending articles.

"No, they'd gone, Maudie, they never came back to the house at all."

"Didn't Mr. Featherstone invite them to tea?"

"I expect he forgot."

"Didn't forget his own tea then," said Maudie in a lower tone, having by that time received the loaded tray and the simple phrase, "He wants his in the study," from Mrs. Pigeon. She set about getting it, while Bertie slumped into a chair at the kitchen table. She was feeling most peculiar suddenly. Her eyes were hot and burning and didn't seem able to focus properly, even her legs were wobbly. Her insides seemed to be empty of more than tea, as though somebody had taken the plug out and left her energy running. Perhaps she was going to be ill. It was almost a comforting thought, as then surely nobody could blame her for anything, she couldn't be expected to manage.

On the other hand that would depend on who was doing the expecting. Human beings fell ill, understood about things like that and made allowances for each other, but would creatures who never fell ill make allowances?

"You do look poorly, dear. You must go to bed really early to-night, so you won't find it so hard to get up. I had such a job waking you this morning I was quite worried. Drink that, dear, it'll do you good."

Bertie steamed her face over the cup of tea offered in almost defiant heresy by Mrs. Pigeon, and felt, in a way, relieved. She wasn't going to be ill. She was simply terribly tired. After all. she had only slept about three or four hours the night before. That had never happened in her life before, and she felt rather proud of it. She began composing another letter to Minty in her head in which she casually put in the remark that she wasn't able to concentrate very well because she had only slept three hours the previous night, and then the letter in her head stopped abruptly as she remembered why. There really was nobody at all to whom she could tell what had happened, nobody who wouldn't think she was joking or mad. Except, perhaps, Maudie, who, returned from the study, was drinking her illegal cup of tea opposite and getting, with sober relish, outside a large piece of Mrs. Pigeon's banished cake.

For a moment she almost toyed with the idea of telling Maudie everything, she would be so excited and absorbed an audience that it was a real temptation. It would be a relief, too, to unload the memory on to someone else, and Maudie might come up with an idea.

"Mr. Featherstone's making such a pretty model in his study, you should see it, really you should. Really clever with his hands he is, even though they do wobble at times with him being so old. He was saying some terrible things when I came in, trying to fix one of the little things that hold it up, you know." Maudie let fall a piece of cake, chased it along the kitchen table, pincered it and, throwing up her head and opening her mouth like a seal at feeding time, dropped it in. "I wish he'd give it to me. I was always fond of doll-sized things. I like miniatures better than pictures, for instance."

It took Bertie in her mazy state a little time to work out what the model must be of; her mind laboriously pictured for her

Great-Uncle Felix playing with a dolls' house, and refused to flash anything else on the screen. She certainly couldn't imagine him swearing, there was something too fastidious about him for that. There were probably quite a few words in his vocabulary that Maudie, not recognising any more than she would herself, might accept as swearing.

"Don't be silly, dear, you can't appreciate what Mr. Featherstone is doing. He's using the principles of engineering." Mrs. Pigeon made it sound as if they were a good substitute for fingers.

"I don't know anything about the principles of engineering," Maudie was inclined to be sulky under Mrs. Pigeon's snubs, "but I do know it was pretty." She pushed her cup forward aggressively for a refill. "And Mr. Featherstone said you were to go to him directly you'd finished." Her voice was softened for Bertie, for whom she evidently felt sympathy. "You can see for yourself then, can't you?"

It was no use putting it off any more. This study thing had to be gone through with. Bertie got up, shook her crumbs on to the table where Maudie eyed them wistfully, and put her cup on the draining-board. Thank goodness, she didn't feel quite so ghastly as she had done. No wonder the British were supposed to have founded their Empire on cups of tea.

Great-Uncle Felix's study door had a silver galleon on it for a knocker, with which she rapped against the panel rather nervously. The "Come in, come in," that followed was both testy and preoccupied and, after closing the door carefully behind her, she saw why.

The walls were panelled in some dark wood so, without being able to see very well, she had the impression of a room cluttered with objects, books, stuffed birds, scrolls, carved figures, maps, globes, pictures, dried flowers, paperweights, pistols, and yet more books, huge, leather-bound ones, some open, piled up crookedly, with paper markers stuck in them. This was all in her peripheral vision, though; right in front of her, sitting with his back to the light coming in through the window, Great-Uncle Felix, moustache screwed up in concentration, tried to insert a matchstick-sized column under the domed roof of a temple the size of a large pepper-pot. It rested on a plaster mound, painted green, which in turn had for its foundation a large tray occupying most of the surface of his desk that was not stacked with books.

"Oh, it's lovely!"

"Don't say anything." She noticed his finger-joints were swollen with rheumatism and, just as Maudie had said, his hands trembled as he worked. The column, however, went in and stayed in. "Now. What was it?"

"You wanted to see me."

"Ah yes, Sit down, sit down." He waved his hand at a chair with three books on it, and the matchstick column, resenting the current of air, fell down. Great-Uncle Felix made a noise like a cat whose tail has been trodden on, seized a pair of tweezers lying on the desk and began a rescue operation. Bertie picked the books off the chair and put them on top of four others on the edge of a table behind her. She drew the chair up to the desk and sat down. The column, drawn out, was gripped with the same intensity that was in the glare directed at her.

"Has no one ever taught you not to fidget about when someone is trying to concentrate?"

Bertie didn't feel there was any future in pointing out that she had been sitting down, not fidgeting, and he had told her to do it.

"Is it the Folly? It does look super."

"Certainly it is the Folly," Great-Uncle Felix's voice was mollified and Bertie reflected that one of the nicest things about him was that he seemed to think her opinion was as important as anyone's. "Neo-classical, of course, with obvious Renaissance influences. Some of it I would like to have in marble, but the problem of transport is considerable."

"They floated the blue stones from Wales to Stonehenge. By river."

Great-Uncle Felix gave this his attention, and then shook his head. "River transport is no longer practicable in these days, I'm afraid, and the cost of labour quite prohibitive. No, I shall have to be content with stone, properly dressed, of course."

She knew that dressed stone was stone with its surface finished in a kind of polish, but all the same she saw the columns demurely clothed in frilly drawers. Great-Uncle Felix saw her face.

83

"Ludicrous, of course, I know it should be marble, you are perfectly right. Nevertheless, I think we must not be too purist over this. A Folly is primarily entertainment, something light-hearted, extravagant, a graceful flourish."

Bertie tried to shut out the memory of the dancers she had seen—was it really only last night? They had been light-hearted and graceful, but everything to do with them had now the quality of nightmare. She looked down at her hands, which were gripping the sides of the chair. To prevent the nightmare getting a hold in her own life, she had to remember, she had to try to do something about what might happen.

"Have you decided to—build it?"

Great-Uncle Felix was squinting through the columns up at the tiny domed roof and she had a disconcerting view of the minor moustache he kept up his nostrils. He didn't seem to have heard her.

"It will be coved, you know. Some *trompe l'oeil* is inevitable in such a limited space, but I fancy the effect will be satisfactory."

He might just as well be talking Double Dutch. How could she make him hear? For that matter, how could she make him do what she wanted and leave the Knowe alone? If she wasn't careful, she would start crying, she was beginning to feel weak and horribly tired all over again. She tried another tack.

"Are you going to let Mr. Pack dig up the Knowe?"

He unfixed the squint and stared at her suddenly through the columns, a giant face against their tininess, and she felt a moment of unreasoning terror. As a child, she had refused to go up a staircase in a big store—was it in High Street, Kensington?—because there were huge figures, twice life-size, painted on the walls.

"Pack? The man is completely ignorant about neo-classicism. I had to explain the simplest architectural term to him——"

And I bet he'd have to explain the simplest archeological term to you, thought Bertie, if you ever let him start anything in that line at all. It was funny how no one ever thought anyone was educated unless they knew something about their own special subject; not too much of course, but just enough to appreciate how clever they were. Great-Uncle Felix had fallen silent in the mind-blowing effort of getting the displaced column back in service. Bertie looked at the plaster mound beneath the model and wondered if it had been made solid, or hollow.

"Are you going to dig a foundation?"

The tweezers, poised, were snatched away with a snort of irritation.

"You had better leave the room, Roberta, if you are going to interrupt with irrelevant questions when I am engaged in such delicate work. Very insensitive!"

Bertie got up, slowly. She had thought it a singularly relevant question, and so would he, if he knew what it really referred to. Was he, or was he not, going to dig into the Knowe in order to throw up sufficient earth to strengthen the foundations of his summerhouse—or temple, it looked a bit like both—was he, in fact, going to break open the Knowe? She felt dizzy again, as though the circle of shadowy faces pressed round her once more in silent threat.

"Roberta! You are rocking the table. If you are going to be so clumsy you had better retire altogether, it would be safer. I cannot have my work in danger!"

Bertie pulled herself together, and took her hands off the table. The model building, with its tiny dome and fragile columns, was indeed swaying slightly in the earthquake she had caused, and Great-Uncle Felix's indignant face behind it watched her out of the room.

"Be careful of the door!"

She resisted the impulse to slam it, and, instead, shut it so noiselessly, taking about a minute to let the lock slide back, that she felt a mouse would have needed a hearing-aid to notice it. As she released the last centimetre of lock she looked up and saw Maudie, in the corridor, staring at her with wide eyes.

"If you've come for his tray, he hasn't even begun."

She remembered a plate of bread and honey she had moved from the top book on the pile on the chair, and there had been a full glass of milk and a packet of wheatgerm among the jumble on his desk. "Anyhow, you'd better not go in, he's busy with his model and doesn't want anyone around."

Maudie spoke hoarsely, evidently impressed with the need for

85

quiet after watching Bertie's burglar-like tactics with the door. "Has he said what it's for? Is he going to put it up somewhere in the garden?"

Clearly the significance of the plaster mound had escaped her. Bertie found the words tumbling out.

"It's for the Knowe, that's the awful thing about it. He's going to put it bang on top of the Knowe!" She could hear her voice rising hysterically, and then the door behind her was jerked open.

"What is this ridiculous noise about? How is it possible for me to concentrate on my Folly while people are jabbering in the corridor? Go away immediately and get on with something useful, both of you!" The door shut sharply.

As Maudie scuttled away, Bertie felt rather as if a glass of cold water had been tossed into her face. She had been about to tell Maudie everything, she realised; and, now she hadn't, felt almost a conviction that Maudie wasn't the right person to tell. Yet there had to be somebody, she had come to the end of any thinking she could do for herself, now she must have advice. Maudie would believe her all right, but she wouldn't be much use in any situation which would bring her up against Great-Uncle Felix, and she might easily get stuck at panic-stations, which would be no joke. Great-Uncle Felix was too far round the twist to reach, Mrs. Pigeon—she wasn't sure about Mrs. Pigeon—she might believe her but even she was scared of her employer. For that matter, who wouldn't be scared of Great-Uncle Felix?

The answer in her own mind was instantaneous and actually stopped her in her tracks as she walked down the corridor. Gawain Pack. If there existed anyone who didn't give a blind, half-witted fig for her Great-Uncle Felix, he was that one.

But was there any use in not being scared of someone if, instead, you drove them so much further round the twist that they couldn't even be sighted on a clear day? On the other hand, Gawain had been terribly useful, so far, in putting Great-Uncle Felix against the idea of having the dig. Was she clever enough to manipulate Gawain so that he could, somehow or other, put Great-Uncle Felix off having his Folly built too?

# CHAPTER

12

Bertie had a vague idea of comforting Maudie who had run from her great-uncle as from Dracula himself, but she was feeling of a sudden so overwhelmingly sleepy that, although she longed above all things to go upstairs and lie down on her bed, it was too impossibly fatiguing to consider. Instead, she made for the first place that looked comfortable, a deep window-seat off the hall, with dusty brown cushions and dusty brown velvet curtains. She curled up in it and partly drew one curtain to shield her from the corridor. Outside, thick laurel bushes made a kind of green twilight through the window. She didn't even attempt to start trying to work out the situation again, there wasn't time before she fell asleep.

In her dreams, all kinds of things were happening, the Folly was being built, only it wasn't the proper size but tiny, as in the model, and there were tiny workmen to match, hauling up the columns, just like an illustration to *Gulliver's Travels* she had once seen. Great-Uncle Felix was giving them orders through a megaphone, but that was all wrong, because he was giant-size and he was too loud for them to hear. He was in some kind of danger, too, she knew that, but she didn't know what it was, so she couldn't warn him. They must be out of doors, or at any rate a wind was blowing, because there were autumn leaves drifting past her face, towards the mound. Now she saw them properly, though, they weren't leaves at all, they were knights in armour, riding on brown horses, but so miniature that they were still the size of the leaves, their armour fluted in tiny scrolls of bronze and gold. She couldn't see their faces, as their visors were down, but their intentions were plain as they bent over the necks of their horses, the lances under their arms, no bigger than golden needles, couched for the attack.

The pleasure she had been feeling in their doll-like perfection was suddenly swallowed up in terror, the silent grip of nightmare. She felt her mouth open, and out of it came a howl with no sound.

She woke up with a jerk, hitting her head on the wooden sill of the window-seat. For a moment she had no idea of where she was; the green twilight, the brown curtains, made nonsense to her, and the fear of her nightmare lay on her like suffocation. Then she managed to move and, as she put her legs down, the curtain she had drawn grated on its rings and she saw the hall beyond. The door of Great-Uncle Felix's study opened and he came out.

But the nightmare somehow, horribly, continued. Great-Uncle Felix was bent over, like an old, old man, with one hand to his hip and the other clinging to the door handle. His face was screwed up, like a man in agony. Bertie felt her own jaw drop, just as in her dream, but this time a noise came out, frightening her.

"Roberta, come here! Stop making that abominable row. Give me your arm and help me upstairs, and then go and get Mrs. Pigeon."

She wasn't sure how she made herself get near the unrecognisable figure, but his voice, that hadn't changed and was as peremptory as ever, helped. She was even able to let him lean on her arm—for such a bony, fragile man he was surprisingly heavy—and to summon up the courage to ask,

"What's happened? Did you fall?"

"Fall? Ridiculous, I am not a dodderer, Roberta. Simply, in my recent preoccupations I have overlooked something vital."

A sudden, blissful hope visited Bertie. He was going to say it would be all wrong to build on the Knowe.

"Absolutely vital, of course. I have neglected my protein-intake,

88

and now my muscles are suffering, naturally. I haven't had an attack like this since I adopted a correct way of eating."

"An attack?"

"Rheumatism, Roberta, rheumatism!" Great-Uncle Felix had turned to glare at her for being so slow, and the movement made him grip the banister in a spasm of pain until the knuckles stood out on his bony hand. But at the word "attack" Bertie had seen the horsemen again, sweeping on, and their golden lances.

This, then, was how they let her know they had not yet lost all their powers. Wasn't that the exact phrase *she* had used, in the Knowe? "Those who interfere we have our own ways of punishing," the cold silver purr was still in Bertie's ears, while her hands were busy supporting Great-Uncle Felix's weight up the stairs. It was obvious that every step hurt him and also obvious that he was fighting the pain. Bertie felt that when he groaned, which he did once or twice, the sound was wrenched out of him, and she was surprised at the strength of the answering surge of sympathy in her. He was her own great-uncle, after all, he was her own kin, he was her own kind, a human being against Them. And he didn't even know what he was fighting against and wouldn't believe her if she told him; it made her both furious and wretched. She had to protect him and she didn't know how to do it.

When she had got him as far as his bedroom and the few steps inside which reached his bed, he collapsed on to it, his face white and shining with sweat, his lips drawn back over his teeth like a cat about to swear. The moustache wasn't aggressive any more, it was a taut scrap of bristle over the pain-stretched mouth. She was going to cry again.

"You shouldn't have made the model, you shouldn't have done it!" She was gulping, roaring, vaguely aware that tears were falling on her hands, probably on Great-Uncle Felix too. His voice, penetrating her roars, was not so much feeble as irritated.

"Great heavens, girl, pull yourself together! You mustn't give way to this hysteria! So bad for me in this state, when I need you to fetch Mrs. Pigeon."

The simple egoism of this helped to steady her. Fetching Mrs. Pigeon was at least something she could do, too, and would get

89

her away from watching Great-Uncle Felix suffering. She rushed out of the room, falling over something on the way—her blurred vision telling her that his bedroom was no less full of strange objects than was his study—and ran blindly down the stairs. She nearly collided with an alarmed Mrs. Pigeon at the bottom.

"What *is* the matter, dear? Have you hurt yourself?"

"No, it's Great-Uncle Felix, he's got terrific pains——"

"Where?" Mrs. Pigeon, looking terrified now, had raised her hands to her heart as if afraid the pains were in that region, and Bertie had a sick moment of wondering if They would have that amount of power. Could They actually kill Great-Uncle Felix? Perhaps, if no one took any notice of the warning. But then, why did They need her at all, if They could hurt, or even get rid of, anyone who attempted to break into the Knowe? There wasn't time to puzzle over this, when she could hear herself gabbling, "Pains all over, he says it's rheumatism, he wants you to go and help, I think he wants some sort of health food to put him right."

"*That* won't put him right in a minute, just like that. Dear me, I've never known him taken ill before, and that's a fact."

Bertie watched Mrs. Pigeon bustle up the stairs, shaking her head. Some of the pins out of her bun were already tinkling on the stairs. It was terrible realising that other grown-ups didn't know what to do, either, when you were dashing to them in an emergency. Always, before, Mother or Daddy had coped, whatever was wrong. They had done the deciding, you didn't have to think, you just had to tell them and then you could give up. Now, nobody in the house knew what was wrong, even, so of course they didn't know what to do, and she, who did know couldn't tell them, and didn't know what to do either.

She couldn't even bear to stay in the house where Great-Uncle Felix was upstairs, like that. She crossed the hall, jerked open the door, and crunched across the drive to the garden. It was a lovely evening, and perhaps the fresh air would clear her head—what with dozing off and crying all over Great-Uncle Felix she had acquired a splitting headache and a feeling that any little nooks and crannies in her nasal passages had been stuffed with hot cotton wool.

It was only about six o'clock and the westering sun had still a lot of warmth in it, which was strangely comforting to her swollen face, when she would have expected a cool breeze would have helped more. She lifted her chin, eyes shut to the point where she could just see where she was going, so she wouldn't walk into anything, and wandered slowly along one of the paths bordered by rose pergolas. From yesterday morning, she remembered that it led down to the walk with the willow-tree seat and, of course, on her left was the yew-hedge enclosing the lawn, the private garden room that had seemed so full of presences. She opened her eyes abruptly. That meant that They were in the garden too, that she couldn't get away from Them anywhere.

How far did Their power extend, anyway? She had just seen a demonstration of what They could do, she was quite sure of that, but maybe there was a limit, maybe rheumatism was the trump card, so to speak. How did one know, though, what was accident and what was Them? If it hadn't been for her dream, she might not have been so sure about what was wrong with Great-Uncle Felix. What she needed was to know a lot more about Them.

She was just going to turn back to the house to look for the library when, at the end of the walk, by the railings that separated it from the meadow, she saw a movement. A tall figure had just passed out of her line of vision.

Bertie felt a sensation roughly as though her stomach had taken a lift to her throat, her heart having preceded it to her ears. She stood for a moment, staring, listening tensely but unable to hear anything but her heart's jumping thud.

The elfstone! Where was it? She couldn't remember when she had last seen it. It must have been in her hand when she went into—was drawn into—the Knowe, but after that dazzling moment she had no idea where it had gone.

Did that mean the figure she had just glimpsed couldn't be *his*? Even though she longed to ask questions, to receive help—and he had, after all, prevented her from taking their food and drink— there was something eerie, other-worldly, about her memory of him that stopped her from going forward to find out.

"Hist!"

Bertie let out a noise in shrillness and urgency like the steam escaping from a boiler and leapt about a foot. Gawain came out of the arch in the yew hedge at her side and made conductor-like gestures in front of her to get her to quieten down.

"For glory's sake, get the pianissimo working! Hist isn't the signal for lift-off, and anyway I bet you haven't checked that space-suit."

"You frightened me!"

"I noticed. There I was, all set to follow up 'Hist' with 'Fear not, gentle maiden' when you went into your expiring peacock stunt. You'd better watch it, even your best friend has to admit your fits are escalating. Come in here."

The long, thin hand on her arm drew her into the enclosed lawn where she would not willingly have gone by herself. "There. I haven't the least wish for your uncle to look out of his window and see the wolf pack in his garden; and pergolas, though pretty, have holes in."

"He wouldn't look out of his window anyway, because he's lying on his bed with violent rheumatism. He can't move."

Gawain raised his eyebrows, but he didn't look unsympathetic. "Rheumatism? Isn't that heresy in the Molasses Belt? I should have thought he could mix himself a stiff yeast and go out and do a rhumba. He was all right this afternoon. Father was saying he could hardly keep up with him."

"Well, he isn't all right now, it's ghastly." Bertie was annoyed with herself for feeling so weepy and for wanting to break down all over Gawain and tell him the lot. Anyone less likely to believe her than the sophisticated Gawain she could hardly imagine.

"Cheer up, it won't last, he'll soon be springing about the countryside having a look at his Folly from all angles."

At that Bertie did another dissolve, aware, furiously, of Gawain's surprised face through the painful blur. She was surprised, herself, to be led to a seat in one of the arbours in the hedge-wall, to be patted quite competently on the back and lent a large, not very clean, tartan handkerchief, smelling of chocolate. She was also fed some of the chocolate it smelt of, while Gawain chewed the rest philosophically at her side.

"I'm sorry. I didn't sleep much last night, and I think I'm feeling a bit funny."

"My dear child." Gawain squinneyed at her. "You really are ill. Why didn't you say?"

"I'm not really ill. It's just that things are going all wrong. I can't explain." She picked at a red and gold thread on the handkerchief. Her eyes must be looking frightful.

Gawain smoothed out the silver paper the chocolate had been wrapped in and tried to fit it over his knee.

"Begin. It's amazing what you can explain once you start. I got last year's Olympic Gold, for explaining at school."

He wasn't looking at her, he was busy moulding the silver paper to his kneecap. She didn't want him to turn round and look at her incredulously or, worse than anything, start laughing. He would probably go back and tell Clothilde, and she would start up her sick cat act.

"You'll only think I'm bonkers."

"Everyone's bonkers. It's just a question of degree. If it's anything to do with your uncle, I'll believe it straight away. He must have got his degree in madness somewhere in the twenties and we're still slaving way behind."

"It's me you'll think mad, not him."

"Go on, I challenge you. I bet you I won't think you're mad. And if you are, I'll pay for a mounted escort and a pipe band all the way to the loony bin——"

"What are you doing here, anyway?" Bertie interrupted, having finally had time to wonder.

"I thought you needed a chum, chum."

Bertie was overwhelmed. He had no idea how much she needed a friend.

"So now prove you're mad."

Bertie didn't know what to say. The sun had left the bench and was beginning to sink below the yew hedge and, although it wasn't late yet, hardly supper time, she was conscious of a slight chill in the air. Memories of last night, and her walk under the moon through the garden and the field to the Knowe, came into her mind. She thought of the twisted face of Great-Uncle Felix, and without working out at all what she was going

93

to say, began to speak jerkily, her fingers plucking at the loose thread in Gawain's handkerchief.

"It's to do with the Knowe. It isn't safe. You know what your sister said?"

"About the Good Folk?"

"What are they?"

"What sensible people call the Fairies. The Greeks called their snake-haired types who haunted you if you bumped off your father the Pleasant Ones. I mean, you don't whizz up to one and say your snakes are looking a bit sick this morning—you pretend hard they only mean well and they'll go away if you shut your eyes and count a-hundred-and-whup. Particularly if you *have* bumped off your father."

"I see. Then if—the Furies, weren't they?—were actually the opposite of pleasant, They—these people I'm talking about— must actually be the opposite of good. They must be evil."

Remembering what she had felt on that lawn, Bertie spoke in a whisper, and so urgently that Gawain dropped his silver paper and turned round to stare at her.

"What on earth has happened?"

"I went inside."

"The *Knowe*?"

"Yes. Last night. This morning, really."

"How?"

"It was that thing Clothilde called the elfstone. It sort of opened it. At midnight."

"What were you doing out there at midnight?"

"I was told to go. You remember you said had I seen anyone hanging round the Knowe when we were talking about it? Well, I didn't say, but I had. He was sent by Them to tell me to come back at midnight, so I did."

"Go on." Gawain was leaning forward now, still staring. Bertie couldn't make out what his expression was.

"And then, as I said, it opened and I went in."

"Simple but effective; and then?"

"Well, She—she was on a sort of throne, and there was dancing all round and music, really lovely, and a marvellous smell of flowers, all fresh—she told me why They wanted me."

94

"For grief's sake, don't leave me guessing."

"I told you you would laugh."

"Lady, I'm not laughing. Why did they want you?"

"They thought I could help. They don't want the Knowe messed about, you see."

"What made them think you could do anything?"

"That's what I couldn't get, either, but apparently I was the only choice because of my age, or something. They can't get through to everyone, and I'm sort of half-way to being grown up and on the wave-length. Do you believe what I'm telling you?"

"I'll wait and see till I've heard it all. What did you say?"

"I said I didn't see what I could do."

"How was that received by the Boss?"

"She wasn't pleased. In fact, I suppose that she threatened. She said They still had powers, and people had forgotten about them but they still worked and people who interfered would get punished."

Gawain whistled. "So that's what you think is wrong with your uncle. Boy, what a story! Build not thy house upon sand, nor thy Folly upon a Knowe."

"What I don't understand, though, is why, if They can punish people, They bothered to try to get hold of me to stop the Knowe being broken into. They could just cripple anyone who tried."

"Maybe that's what happened to my poor old Fa when he slipped a disc in Egypt two years ago. Curse of the Mummy on Daddy. Still, it didn't stop him from going on with the excavations, even though he had to tell everyone what to do from flat on his back. If you ask me, it takes more than a nasty accident or two to put an archaeologist off his dig. I'll grant you, they may drop dead eventually but by then the digging has been done. But—boy, what a story. Wait till Clothilde hears this."

Bertie's heart sank. She had been feeling really glad that she had told someone, relieved at getting it off her chest, grateful that Gawain hadn't just fallen about but had listened to everything she said. And now he was going to go home, exactly as she had feared, and laugh himself sick telling that supercilious sister of his. She took hold of his sleeve and shook it, without thinking. He looked down at his arm as she did it.

"Don't tell her. Please; I don't want you to tell her. She won't believe it and she'll just laugh. You'll both make fun of me, I know you will." She was half crying again, the handkerchief had fallen on the bench between them and Gawain picked it up and offered it back. He was smiling too, quite nicely.

"O.K. I will preserve the beans from spilling. If Clothilde ever finds out, mind, what I've been keeping from her, she'll make me sit and help while she flays me alive. It's so totally up her street, she's mad about this sort of folk stuff."

Bertie, using the handkerchief, stopped and looked at him over the top of it. "What do you think it is? Just a story? Do you think I'm mad?" It was dreadfully important to know. If he thought she was mad, her last hope of any help was gone.

He didn't answer her directly, and her courage took another blow. He had retrieved the silver paper from the grass at their feet and with one long finger made a spyhole in the middle of it, through which he gravely peered at the view.

"It's an interesting story. You want to know if I think it's true? My dear Bertie, truth is relative, someone must have told you that by now. If I saw the whole world through silver paper, for instance, my view might be limited, or decorated, or whatever, but it would be perfectly true. A scientist might come along and try to open up your Knowe with the flint, elfstone—where is it now, by the way?"

Bertie tried again to think. Her mind didn't want to go back to what had happened—was it really only that morning? The stone itself didn't seem very important now, but what had she done with it?

"I think I must have dropped it inside."

"Pity. I'd have liked to have a look at it."

"You did. Don't you remember you saw the man at the window in your sitting-room—the one who wasn't there when we got outside? That was when you took it from my hand."

Gawain put down the paper and looked at her thoughtfully.

"You mean, you think it was the same man who appeared to you at the Knowe to tell you to come? This gets curiouser and curiouser." He seemed to be enjoying the idea, Bertie noticed with

96

a lightening of the heart. "But it's still a pity about the stone. Evidence, you know. The scientist would want to test it."

"I don't think," said Bertie firmly, "that the scientist would be allowed to test it if They didn't want him to."

"Could be you're right." Gawain took hold of a quantity of his hair, which he wore rather long, and gave it a reflective tug as if to see whether or not it would come away. "The problem now being, what are we going to do about all this? We must try——"

He was interrupted by the faint but sonorous sound of the dinner-gong from the house—Mrs. Pigeon must be beating it out of the window, Bertie thought, from the noise—and stood up, unfolding himself from the bench in instalments. Bertie had already jumped up and was looking at him wordlessly. There wasn't any need any more to ask him if he believed her.

Bertie was very reluctant to see Gawain go just when for the first time she felt she might get some help. She didn't doubt that he would have to go, as it must be about his dinner-time too, and his father and sister and whoever cooked for them—Bertie put an apron on Clothilde in her imagination, and hastily took it off again—would be waiting for him. In her world parents always wanted to know what you were doing and where you were, and liked to get definite invitations at parent-level for their children. Not, it appeared, in Gawain's world.

"If that's noshing-time, why don't I stay, and we can work out a Plan."

"But——" Bertie didn't quite know how to put it.

"Your uncle won't have me under his roof in case it falls on me as a punishment from Heaven? O.K., but isn't he in bed? If his rheumatism is that bad, he won't tackle the stairs again. If his eye doesn't see me, his heart won't grieve over me."

"Mrs. Pigeon might tell him." In her heart, Bettie did not think this likely. There was already, as far as she could see, quite a lot that Mrs. Pigeon didn't tell him, and she certainly wasn't a trouble-maker.

"We'll ask her then." Gawain took her by the arm and steered her out of the enclosed lawn, through the arch in the tall hedge and across the rose walk towards the back of the house. The sun was very low by now, and its level golden-rosy light made the bricks glow and the Tudor window-panes glitter. There was a soft breeze blowing, enough to ruffle the hair lightly and carry the scent of the roses past them as though the garden were breathing peacefully before settling to sleep. Going up the steps of the terrace with Gawain, Bertie felt a sudden rush of happiness, as though her luck had turned and, somewhere, a move had been made in her favour. She still felt exhausted, she was still worried about Great-Uncle Felix, she had anxieties even deeper than that about which she wouldn't let herself think, but at least she wasn't alone.

Mrs. Pigeon was delighted that Gawain wanted to stay to supper, she seemed to think it was a way of making up for the lack of hospitality shown earlier in the day when the Packs had so signally not been invited to tea. Supper, Bertie was glad to see, was going to be in the kitchen, not the dining-room, and to judge from the spread on the table, to which Mrs. Pigeon was liberally adding, from cupboards, tins, and the fridge, the food itself was not going to conform too strictly to her great-uncle's standards of what was, and was not, poisonous. There was, for instance, the rest of the gorgeous chocolate cake she had had a slice of at tea, and a plate of hot sausage rolls, among other things (flaky pastry was a blasphemy to Great-Uncle Felix, she was sure), and a splendid (white) bread-and-butter pudding. Bertie had never seen a pudding at Longbarrow yet, only fruit, but she had heard her great-uncle say that a whole-grain rice pudding was very nourishing, if it were taken with molasses. She wondered if Mrs. Pigeon had made the pudding for herself and Maudie to eat in secret in the kitchen, or in a hurry, for Bertie as well, when she knew Great-Uncle Felix would not be coming down to dinner. As she thought this, she was shocked that she hadn't even asked how he was, but Gawain, at that minute, was doing what she should have done.

"How is Mr. Featherstone now?"

Mrs. Pigeon paused in the opening of a tin of baked beans (all the tins came out of a high cupboard she had to stand on a chair to get at; presumably, she hoped too high for Great-Uncle Felix's long arms to investigate), to rescue a hairpin that was being slowly squeezed out of her bun. She seemed to take to Gawain,

Bertie noticed, and he didn't have, with her, that wildly infuriating way of talking that got her great-uncle's goat so successfully and kept that animal fully engaged.

"Really bad, he is, I've never known him like it. Says the pain is going through him like knives all the time, just as though someone were sticking needles into him. I wanted him to get the doctor, but Mr. Featherstone never would have a doctor in the house if he could help it. Last time Dr. Houghton came, Mr. Featherstone was so short with him he just snapped his bag shut and walked out, he did, saying he wouldn't come here any more, not if Mr. Featherstone was dying." Mrs. Pigeon shook the beans into the saucepan with a satisfying slosh. "Very quick-tempered, Dr. Houghton, too."

Gawain's face didn't change, but Bertie was sure he was enjoying the idea of the two men glaring at each other as much as she was. He was already lounging at the kitchen table, his legs stretching apparently half across the room. Maudie, to whom he had nodded pleasantly when he came in, had done some washing up since then almost entirely without the aid of her eyes and with her head turned over her shoulder towards Gawain.

"This is a super spread, Mrs. Pigeon. I haven't seen anything like this for years."

Mrs. Pigeon flushed, shed a hairpin and beamed.

"Now you're just saying that to be polite."

(Bertie wondered what her great-uncle would have made of this accusation directed at Gawain.)

"Seriously, Mrs. Pigeon, I'd be lucky to get bread and cheese tonight. Saturday's Rita's night off, and my sister hurls the meal together if she feels like it. Mostly we get anything that's going—or that hasn't actually gone off."

"Oh, that's terrible! You poor things!" Mrs. Pigeon, shocked, piled the beans on his plate, and Maudie, with wistful pity in her eyes, sighed, and felt for the draining-board with the cup. "At your age you're still growing, and you should get plenty to eat. If you'll excuse me saying so, you're far too thin as it is."

"Do you think so?" Gawain looked at his skinny wrists complacently before he took knife and fork and set about demolishing his beans and toast. "I often think," he remarked with his mouth full, a few minutes later, "that Father could drape me with a necklet or two and claim he'd dug me up somewhere. The sort of thing he hopes to find in the Knowe here."

He caught Bertie's eye and solemnly shut one of his own, but Mrs. Pigeon was blind to all such subtleties. She started violently and dropped the cake-tin she was holding, while Maudie, not to be outdone in noise and confusion, missed the draining-board with a plate. Gawain ate calmly through the clangour, crashing, and exclamations, and was helping himself to sausage rolls by the time order was restored and the pieces picked up.

"Mr. Pack's not really going to do his archaeology here, is he?" Mrs. Pigeon's voice indicated what a very unsavoury performance she thought it would be. "I wouldn't have thought Mr. Featherstone would ever have allowed it, from what he's said. There's that funny building he wants up on it, too, where's that to go if it's all dug up?"

"Anyway," Maudie's contribution came out in a low squeak, and she turned scarlet when Gawain looked at her over his second sausage roll, "anyway, it's dangerous, it really is. Someone should tell your Dad."

"Dangerous in what sense? That the whole construction will founder at the touch of a spade and my father will be in among the grave goods with his own contribution of loose vertebrae?"

"You know what I mean. They won't like it. Then your Dad will get taken ill like Mr. Featherstone, you'll see."

Gawain took the last sausage-roll, and looked at Bertie. "You may be right, Maudie, but as I told Bertie, you don't put an archaeologist off his dig that easily. In any case, Mr. Featherstone hardly gave my father any encouragement this afternoon. As Mrs. Pigeon says, you can't dig up the Knowe *and* put a Folly on it."

"But," Mrs. Pigeon anxiously opened another cake-tin and revealed an unsuspected hoard of further sausage-rolls, "it doesn't look as though Mr. Featherstone is going to be able to do any building in his condition."

"If you ask me," said Maudie from the sink as she swilled out the washing-up water with a dismissive gurgle, "nobody's going to do anything at all. They aren't going to be allowed."

None of them said anything more for a bit. Gawain and Bertie ate steadily, Mrs. Pigeon struggled to put up her hair, Maudie stacked the cups and plates. It seemed as though the conclusive remark had been made; Bertie's almost cheerful mood began to be tinged with despair again. Maudie was shrewder than any of them; she had seen the whole point about it all, that they were helpless. There was no use in having Gawain on her side—what could Gawain do, however intelligent he was, against that re-membered Presence in the Knowe and her impossible commands? She took a grip of the edge of the kitchen table. It was important not to start crying again, especially in front of Maudie. Mrs. Pigeon had seen her bawling already and no doubt thought she was upset because of her father. Not that she wasn't, but all that didn't bear thinking about.

A hideous tintinnabulation made them all jump. Mrs. Pigeon threw the cake-tin on the floor and clutched her starting bun. Maudie gave a sharp cry and stepped back against Gawain's tilted chair. He, whether or not unaffected by the noise, could not fail to be affected by the action and was precipitated forward into the chocolate cake from which he had been in the act of choosing a slice. Bertie, who had shrieked a little herself, could not help pressing her hands to her own face at the sight of Gawain's.

"You look like a coal-miner."

"A very welcoming cake."

"It's Mr. Featherstone's bedroom bell. It always gives me such a turn. It makes more noise even than the others."

The still vibrating bell accused them as they picked up the cake-tin, disentangled themselves from chairs, wiped faces and generally restored calm.

"I'll go, Mrs. Pigeon. I never did collect his tea tray."

"No, dear, I'll go. When he's not well like this I think I'd better go. There might be something he'd want and you might not know where to get it. I'm used to his ways, dear."

Bertie thought it was very kind of Mrs. Pigeon to put it like that. Maudie was being brave to suggest going when it was obvious she found Great-Uncle Felix terrifying. Bertie only hoped that when she started her nursing she never ran into a patient like him, or she might give up on the spot. The milk of human kindness, which Maudie evidently had to make her want to take up nursing at all, could last only so long before it turned. It occurred to Bertie that Mrs. Pigeon had managed not to criticise her employer too, which must be pretty difficult for someone who had to bear the brunt of his fads and fancies.

As Mrs. Pigeon was bustling out of the door another bell set up its whirring clatter. Bertie wondered for a minute why Mrs. Pigeon permitted the shock to the system given by all those old-fashioned calyxes hanging above their labels on the wall, before she realised that it would be her great-uncle, who didn't have to answer or hear the bells, who would be the one to permit them. This one said "Front Door" and hardly got the same reaction.

"You see who it is, Maudie, will you? I can't think who'd be calling at this hour."

Bertie was still watching Gawain taking his revenge on the chocolate cake when Maudie burst in on them again.

"It's your father! It's Mr. Pack!" Visitors were of an order of drama that Maudie enjoyed.

"My father." Gawain put the lid over the mangled remains of the cake. "Not like him to visit sick-beds."

"He won't know Great-Uncle Felix is sick. You didn't."

"True. Let's go and see what gives."

What gave was Mr. Pack, blandly looming in the hall, apparently quite vague as to his mission. "What brings *you* here, Dad?"

"I could ask you the same. Hallo, Roberta."

Gawain struck a pose, hand before mouth, that Bertie recognised from seeing a Restoration play as being an aside.

"He little knows why I am here. Dad, if you've come to see the Grand Cham he's in bed with a touch of plumbago. Not feeling very hospitable, I imagine."

"Oh, I'm sorry to hear that."

"It came on very suddenly." Bertie felt compelled to offer that, as an awful thought struck her that perhaps Mr. Pack might think it was a sort of "Not at Home" excuse. She was furious with herself for actually blushing.

"In that case, you know, it might be a slipped disc. It often happens in my line of life, archaeologists are very prone, with all that stooping."

"Slaving over a hot grave. Myself, I think it's natural, one's spine giving way when it sees someone's vertebrae laid out neatly with only a few necklaces for company. Why bother to keep in touch?"

Bertie had noticed before that, apart from tactfully trying to deflect his son's witticisms from homing in on Great-Uncle Felix, Mr. Pack didn't really acknowledge their existence as jokes. No doubt Clothilde's expiring-hen act soothed Gawain's soul; Bertie knew how frightful it was when you'd said something funny and nobody took any notice.

"Mr. Featherstone wants to know who—oh, it's you, Mr. Pack!"

Mrs. Pigeon stood at the top of the stairs, looking muddled, while Mr. Pack unexpectedly covered the distance between them with strides that took in two steps at a time. He put a broad hand on her shoulder and patted it kindly.

"You mustn't worry, Mrs. Pigeon——"

"But he won't see a doctor, Mr. Pack." Bertie repressed the thought that Mrs. Pigeon looking tearfully up, her stout figure divided at the waist by her apron, resembled a hot-cross bun in difficulties. "What am I to do?"

"Leave it to me. I don't think he needs a doctor. I think he needs an osteopath, from the sound of it. Will it be all right if I go and see him?"

Politeness struggled with truth in Mrs. Pigeon's face. "Well, I don't think he's in a very good mood for visitors, Mr. Pack, he's rather edgy, you know."

"A good description of a cut-throat razor," Gawain murmured in Bertie's ear.

"It takes two to make a quarrel, Mrs. Pigeon, and I can recommend him to a very good osteopath."

"It's true," Gawain's voice parted the hair on Bertie's neck. "When Dad came back from Egypt two years ago in the mummy position, feet first, this fellow got him into crouching order in no time."

"Well, if you really think that, Mr. Pack, it's a dreadful responsibility . . ." Mrs. Pigeon was already being ushered down the corridor, blotted from view by the towering Mr. Pack, and they heard a door open and shut. Gawain started for the staircase.

"I'm going to be in on this. Come on."

"But we *can't*. He'll be furious." Bertie's stomach turned over at the thought of witnessing a row between Great-Uncle Felix and Mr. Pack; it had been bad enough his getting cross that afternoon with Gawain. What he would do if Gawain burst into his bedroom now might escalate the whole thing on to a nuclear scale. As Gawain continued to bound up the stairs in a fair imitation of his father, she ran up after him.

"Which is his bedroom?"

"Please don't go in." There she went, clutching at his sleeve again. He turned to look at her and Bertie saw his expression change though she couldn't have said what the change was.

"O.K. Relax. Drop anchor. Take off the skids. We'll wait and see what happens."

Bertie leant against the wall and found she was trembling.

"Why is your father here, anyway?"

"You heard me ask him, and you may have heard him not reply. That's Dad all over. Sly to a fault, think his loving off-spring."

"You mean——"

"I mean he's up to something. Dad may appear to breeze hither and yon, but if you look closely he's always breezing *after* something. He was here only this afternoon, if he's here again it's because he's got another idea and can't wait to try it."

"You mean about the Knowe?"

"That's the lodestar of Dad's life at the moment. He's like that when he hears the Bronze Age calling him. Talk about the horns of Elfland faintly blow—Oh Gawd, I'd forgotten."

The incredible thing was, as she had noticed before, that she could forget too, in spite of what she had seen. No wonder it was tough passing exams, given the state of the human memory. She returned Gawain's stricken gaze and had time to notice, quite irrelevantly, how grey his eyes were, when they both heard voices raised, and Mrs. Pigeon came scurrying past, so upset she didn't question their presence in the corridor,

"Oh dear, I knew he wouldn't like it, I knew he wouldn't! You can't make Mr. Featherstone do anything he doesn't want to do, I could have told Mr. Pack that—now he wants his yeast directly, I'd better not leave it to Maudie, she never can mix it the way he likes . . ."

Mrs. Pigeon talked herself down the stairs. As the green baize door swung to behind her Gawain beckoned to Bertie and tiptoed towards the bedroom door which Mrs. Pigeon had not completely closed. The raised voice from inside, belonging to Great-Uncle Felix, was quite distinct.

"No amount of pictures, Pack, from any journal you care to produce" (Gawain and Bertie exchanged glances) "will convince me that there'd be any point in allowing a wretched bulldozer on to my land to dig up what is a very pleasing elevation, which could be further improved by the addition of an elegant structure——"

"There would be no question of a bulldozer, Featherstone, as you must know. The techniques of excavation are refined ones, we are more likely to be using teaspoons and paintbrushes in the last stages than anything else."

Bertie thought the use of the present tense a little tactless from Mr. Pack, and it was in fact followed by a loud snort from Great-Uncle Felix.

"Quite immaterial to state what you use when you won't be using them. I want to make it perfectly clear what the position is——" The speaker had evidently tried to alter his own position to do so; Bertie imagined him pulling himself up on the pillows, but he interrupted his words by a sharp cry which made her wince in sympathy. Mr. Pack's voice carried smoothly on.

"It seemed to me that, placed as you are at the moment, you might prefer to let us conduct this dig *before* you construct your Folly. I imagine it would not be too difficult to arrange it so the top of the Knowe was left undisturbed, and the grave-chamber beneath excavated in such a way that there would be no great alteration in appearance."

There was a silence in which Great-Uncle Felix could almost be heard thinking. Bertie was filled with terror suddenly, the memory of the hostile, beautiful faces pressing round her came back so that she could feel them round her again, even there. This was the moment. If he decided now to let the Knowe be dug up, he might be a cripple for life, he might have a heart-attack, something might happen to her for not stopping it, or, and her mind swerved past the things she dared not look at, to her mother and father. Daddy might not recover properly from the accident, Mother might really leave him this time . . . She held her breath and gripped Gawain's arm without caring she was doing it.

"You say you think this can be arranged?" Great-Uncle Felix's voice was reflective, and Bertie put the knuckles of one hand into her mouth and bit them.

"I don't see any reason why not. And if we were to recover any grave goods of the sort I was showing you—and, if you remember, the article said there was a definite possibility of a chieftain buried somewhere in this area, and we might well find gold ornaments that would be valuable as well as full of interest archaeologically speaking—then I would suggest when they find their way to a museum they be shown under the title of the "Featherstone Treasure", with suitable acknowledgements to your generosity in permitting the dig."

There was a longer silence this time and Bertie found her knuckles were hurting. Gawain had his head right on the crack between door and jamb and she could see the electric switch on the bedroom wall just beyond. Great-Uncle Felix was speaking in tones of satisfaction.

"Of course, of course. Naturally I can't give too much of my time in interviews, but the papers would expect something. I might write an article myself. They can hardly fail to be interested in my Folly."

This was it. Bertie closed her eyes. She wouldn't have been surprised, at that moment, to hear a clap of thunder and a scream from the room beyond. What she did hear, unexpectedly, was Gawain's voice, and she opened her eyes to find he had pushed the door wider and slipped in, exposing her to the view of her uncle, propped up in bed facing her and looking rather like an illustration to Don Quixote. Mr. Pack beside him had, for once, an expression. It was unwelcoming.

"Hello, Mr. Featherstone. Just came to congratulate you about the dig. Pity you've had to hand over to Dad now you're *hors de combat*, so to speak."

The rising wind of anger had blown Great-Uncle Felix's moustache nearly vertical and he was struggling to speak when Gawain went on, airily evading his father's hand which, surprisingly, had gone out to grasp him, and wandering round the room, hands in pockets.

"These your plans for the Folly, Mr. Featherstone? It's going to look a bit funny perched up on a grave-chamber, isn't it, like a butterfly on a tombstone, rather. I expect the papers will have their little joke about that, as papers will. I can think of one or two who are mad about the bizarre, and they'll really eat this. The Funeral Folly, Charm and Charnel, this way to the Teahouse Tomb. You'll have to keep a scrapbook."

Several things happened at once after this; Great-Uncle Felix made a noise like an airgun going off and, in trying to rise from his pillows, no doubt with the intention of physically annihilating Gawain, followed it up with a roar of pain as he clutched at the bedside table to save himself from falling out of bed, and succeeded in casting everything on the table, in the way of notebooks, glasses of milk and what looked like blackcurrant syrup, a telephone and a paperweight, to the floor in an avalanche of noise and confusion. Mr. Pack had sprung forward to catch Great-Uncle Felix and received instead the paperweight on his foot, which caused him to hop about, contributing his own roars. Bertie, still in the doorway, also hopped, with her hand over her mouth, and Gawain clung to the curtains at the window, yelping with laughter. Mrs. Pigeon had arrived with the yeast and dodged about behind Bertie, uttering faint shrieks and juggling with the glass and spoon on its saucer.

Great-Uncle Felix, with the elasticity of the old, recovered first and, with what Bertie thought was his usual unfairness, turned on Mr. Pack.

"Stop making that appalling row, it's perfectly childish." He turned a bloodshot glare on Gawain beyond, still giving Pekinese cries in the folds of the curtains. "You can take your son and leave this house. I don't wish to hear any more of this digging rubbish again. In fact, I shall send for my lawyer tomorrow and make it a condition in my Will that the Knowe shall *never* be subject to excavation of any nature whatsoever."

Mr. Pack, who had listened to this still clutching his foot, put it to the ground with a grimace when Great-Uncle Felix had finished, picked up the paperweight that had crippled him and set it back with a reverberating thud on the bedside table, seized Gawain's arm, and made for the doorway hastily vacated by both Bertie and Mrs. Pigeon. As Gawain was dragged past, he raised a victorious thumb at Bertie.

She found she was smiling idiotically; he had deliberately set out to help her. She didn't know how much store he set on being on good terms with his father, but he had certainly sacrificed his father's goodwill, however temporarily, to act as a friend to her. In a daze of relief, she half heard Mr. Pack and Gawain clattering down the stairs and Mrs. Pigeon clucking over Great-Uncle Felix.

"Oh Mr. Featherstone, I *am* so glad you're not going to let them do any of their digging here. I was so afraid they might."

"Not even over my dead body. My lawyer shall see to that. I shall telephone him tonight."

"But are you going to dig it up yourself, Mr. Featherstone, to put your building on it?" Mrs. Pigeon was being very daring and Bertie held her breath. This was the essential question. What use to stop the Knowe being dug up by any archaeologist, if it were going to be dug up to provide the foundations of the Folly?

"I shall show Pack, with his so-called refined methods, his teaspoons and paintbrushes, forsooth, that I am capable of similar refinement. The structure I am contemplating has never been a gross one, and should require no more than a platform, to be erected on the mound and possibly grassed over and planted with suitable ferns. That would also," Great-Uncle Felix brightened, his eyes far away and contemplating an inner vision, "give the extra elevation I need. Positively no digging. The idea is absurd, on the level of such earthy clods as the Packs."

This meant, finally, that They would not be disturbed; and Gawain was the one she had to be grateful to. Her mind was whirling with something she couldn't believe had happened. Positively no digging.

"Roberta! Don't stand there gawping but come here."

Great-Uncle Felix fixed her with a bloodshot but sparkling eye over his glass of brewers' yeast and apple-juice. Quarrelling obviously stimulated him. She stood by the bed obediently, her mind wandering off to the Knowe; would They be aware at this moment of what had taken place?

"Now understand this, Roberta. I will not have you encouraging that uncouth young scoundrel—or, for that matter, that opinionated old fake his father—to set foot in my house again. Are you following me?"

He sat up suddenly on his pillows in one of the impatient movements she had come to recognise as preceding a little speech. He had opened his mouth and almost begun to speak when Mrs. Pigeon burst in.

"Oh sir, you must be careful! You know how it hurts you to move."

"Rubbish, Mrs. Pigeon! It does *not* hurt me to move"— Bertie thought she detected a fleeting look of surprise when he said this—"I do not wish to be fussed over in a totally unnecessary way. In fact, I shall dine downstairs."

With Mrs. Pigeon staring over her clasped hands, he swivelled his legs smartly off the bed and put his feet to the floor. Glancing triumphantly at them both he stood up and, walking through the objects that still lay scattered on the floor, twitched into place the folds of the curtains disarranged by Gawain's helpless laughter.

"You're all right, Mr. Featherstone! You've recovered!"

"Of course. If you lead a basically fit life, these muscular weaknesses are only momentary. In future, Mrs. Pigeon, I shall arrange a new diet sheet, concentrating more on proteins. This must not happen again."

Just as if it were *our* fault, thought Bertie, as he stalked out of the room and down the stairs. Mrs. Pigeon came and stood beside her, looking at his retreating figure.

"It must have been a slipped disc after all, dear, and the sudden movement must have slipped it back. We have a lot to be thankful for."

# CHAPTER

## 14

Great-Uncle Felix had to dine alone, however. Bertie explained that she had already had supper, and earned a keen glance from under the frosty eyebrows.

"You have kept to your diet sheet, I trust?"

"You haven't given me one yet, actually." It was an extraordinary thought that she had only been there two days and so much had happened already. There hadn't really been time to get diet-sheets. Great-Uncle Felix seemed put out, more by his lack of memory than her lack of guidance, Bertie thought.

"I can't imagine why I haven't given it to you, it's all drawn up and ready. You had better go to my study and fetch it. No, on second thoughts, don't, you might knock something over. I will fetch it myself, later."

He addressed himself dismissively to some shredded lettuce. Bertie lingered for a moment in the dining-room doorway, partly to see the moustache swing into action, partly because she wasn't sure what he meant her to do, stay and demurely keep him company, or clear out. He looked up again, and a trail of lettuce, revolving, was sucked in to its doom.

"You look tired, Roberta. It has been a long and trying day, very trying indeed to anyone of any sensitivity. I find it almost unbelievable we should have been subjected to such intolerable impertinence. I suggest you take a quick walk round the garden,

get some fresh air into your lungs, and then go to bed. Good-
night."

He forked some more lettuce on to his plate and set to. Bertie
closed the door, and wandered into the hall. She was certainly
fantastically tired, the old boy would never know just how tired,
but the idea about a quick walk round the garden was more than
she wanted at this moment. A quick walk up the stairs to bed was
more like it. She was half-way up when the dining-room door
opened.

"Where are you going, Roberta?"

"It's getting cold, I was just going for my blazer."

She got it. It wasn't on the floor of her room, where she supposed she had left it with all her other clothes when she got back
that morning, but hanging up in the wardrobe, where Mrs.
Pigeon must have put it. It was twilight in her room, the mirror
glimmered at her, paler than the window, the bed invited, from
under its dusky canopy. More than anything, she wanted to forget
the confusion of the day in sleep, to get out of having to think
out the next move, of having to think, even, if there was a next
move, or if the game was mercifully over.

She was standing, asleep on her feet, in the middle of the room
when she felt it. The elfstone was in her pocket, after all.

"Roberta!"

She let go of the elfstone, and the things in her room, which
had started to waver and slip their moorings, went back to normal.

"Coming!"

I know what Great-Uncle Felix did in the war, Bertie said to
herself savagely as she partly shut the door on her finger. He
was one of those men who stand in towers in concentration camps
swivelling a gun over the horizon.

He was standing at the foot of the stairs as she came down,
fixing her with a glare just as good as a gun, any day.

"You must get out of these habits of dawdling, Roberta. They
enfeeble the will. I cannot emphasise too strongly the importance
of exercise in the open air before retiring to sleep. The oxygen
level in the blood is raised, and healthful rest ensues. Even at
your age the muscles need constant exercise to keep them in good
trim, so that when you come to my age you may avoid, with

the help of a balanced diet, the sort of thing that happened today, or, if it should happen, throw it off as successfully as I did." He squared his shoulders, military-fashion, as she passed.

She went through the lobby, dark with overgrown geraniums and full of wellingtons and mackintoshes, conscious of the gun trained on her back from the tower. Nothing else would have sent her out, into that twilight, with the elfstone in her pocket, not knowing what might be waiting for her in the garden beyond.

When her eyes got used to it, the light was stronger outside than she had thought in the house, but the shapes of things were blurred at the edges, and she was uncomfortably reminded of the way the yews had looked last night on the way to the Knowe. She wouldn't go near them to-night.

Her best route, for this quick walk Great-Uncle Felix was no doubt timing by the clock in the hall, was on the path which roughly bordered the garden, dividing it from the fields and woods and from the yew-trees in the formal part at the back. That way, too, she could go round, not through, the secret lawn in the centre, where she had felt, rather than seen, them dancing. She doubled her fists in her pockets and started to trudge round, deliberately making her mind as much of a blank as possible.

She even looked the other way when she got to the tall hedge that protected the lawn, and her footsteps quickened, but after all, it was no use. In turning her head, she didn't see where she was, so when a branch of willow hanging over the path touched her cheek, she stumbled violently, and in her pocket the elfstone jerked into her opened hand. When she turned her head, in that same instant, he was standing there.

Although she had worked out that he was probably human, it didn't really help. He had come from Them.

In the growing dusk his face was not clear, but she felt the sadness coming from him so strongly she could almost have touched it. His voice sounded in her head.

"You must come to them again."

"Why?" Bertie was swamped with terror.

"That you may answer to what they ask."

"Don't they know what goes on?"

113

"Not all that passes everywhere." His hand moved like a shadow in the dusk. "They can hear the grass grow in that field, but between walls their hearing is clouded with things of human make."

"I've done my best." She was practically crying now, her tiredness and the idea of having to go through all the nightmare of the Knowe again took away any strength she had left. "They're not going to dig up the Knowe, he won't let them, he said he'd put it in his will and everything . . ."

"That they have heard, and it is well for you and for him that it is so."

She hiccuped on a sob, and remembered Great-Uncle Felix getting spryly off the bed.

"Then why do they want to see me, and ask me things?"

"So they may reward you according to your wish."

Reward her! It was impossible to think of them as giving favours, doing anything other than threatening and punishing. Another idea occurred to her.

"But it wasn't really me, it was Gawain——"

"You were the reason why he spoke."

She digested this. Even in the middle of her turmoil, it was a nice thought.

"But—a reward! What could they give?" In some of the stories she had read as a child, there had been gold given that had turned to dead leaves the next day.

"Have you no desire close to your heart?"

Her mind jumped immediately to Daddy. Could they make him absolutely better after the accident, make him and Mother get on all right again so they would never, never divorce? After all, she had been afraid, at the worst moments of being afraid, when she hadn't dared to think what she was afraid of, that everything to do with that would go wrong. Even now, she wasn't going to let her fear get as far as actual pictures of what could happen.

She was suddenly aware of him standing there, only a dark shape by now, but patient, and so terribly sad. Something of her own sadness made her say impulsively,

"What about you? Did they give you what you wanted?"

He was silent for a moment, and she had to strain to hear when he did reply.

"What I thought I wanted they gave. I took their food. But it was in another country and long ago."

"Did that put you in their power—the food, I mean?"

"It closed the gates into your world, which was once mine. If you had taken their food last night, you could have moved among your kind as you did today, but after you had done their bidding you would have had to go back into their world, where I am now."

It was a terrifying thought. The voice was almost inaudible now, and unconsciously she clenched her hand on the elfstone. His shape was there still, and had got no dimmer, so perhaps— the thought flashed across her mind—he just didn't want Them to hear? She lowered her own voice to a tiny whisper.

"Can't you get back?"

She must have made her whisper too low, because there was no answer. Of course, just as the biology teacher was always saying, you become what you eat. If you eat food from another world, you become part of that world, and you're stuck with it. No wonder he was sad.

"Isn't there anything you can do?" She whispered a bit louder this time, though now she thought he just hadn't replied because he felt it was hopeless.

Again the silence, and she could feel reluctance now, with the sadness. The voice in her head was very far away.

"Only you can help."

She hadn't expected that, though she supposed she should have. Who else had been inside the Knowe, after all, and knew what he was up against? Cowardly, she wished she had never asked the question, and then she was ashamed. Hadn't he warned *her* about not taking the food?

"What could I do?" It cost her an effort to ask, and an effort not to block the answer that came, not immediately, but after a pause, as if he considered.

"They will grant you a wish."

"You mean I should wish for you?" Oh, that wasn't fair, she thought, there's Daddy and the things I really want. It was her turn to be silent. He doesn't want to ask me, and I made him.

It's probably his only chance, and I might have been the same as him if he hadn't helped. Daddy might be better already, and Mother's last letter wasn't too bad, they seemed to be getting on all right. Bertie wasn't sure that she wanted to think it was They who had helped her with that.

"Would it be enough, wishing for you?"

"They will be angry. They will not let me go easily."

The terror returned, and all she wanted to do was to throw the elfstone from her, as far as she could, and run back to the house.

"You must lay hold of me, to draw me into your world. Do not slacken your grasp, however I may change——"

"Roberta!"

She started at the sound of her Great-Uncle's voice, and the elfstone started with her, out of her fingers. It was baffling to see nothing but the hedge in front of her, to have the voice in her head cut off, as though someone had turned the knob on a transistor. Great-Uncle Felix came up, his feet crunching on the gravel.

"Roberta, it is high time you came in. You cannot go wandering about the garden at night, you know."

Was she imagining it, or did he sound a little alarmed?

"What's wrong with the garden at night?"

"There is nothing wrong with the garden at night, of course. Only a child would think so. I have no intention of letting you roam about, frightening yourself."

"But why should I——"

"If you can fancy that you see people walking about in the garden at twilight——"

Bertie, driven by a sort of rage or despair, took her great-uncle's bony fingers and pressed the elfstone into them. As she did so, there was, immediately, someone who made a third, standing in front of the hedge. She was relieved, in a curious way, that he had not gone.

Great-Uncle Felix was trembling, she could feel the vibration of his body as she held the elfstone between his fingers.

"Get out of my garden, sir! Didn't I tell you never to show your face again here? You and your father have insulted me beyond any apology. I refuse to accept it, I refuse to accept it!"

Of course, he thought any tall young man in the dusk would be Gawain, he was hardly as geared to the supernatural as she was. All the same, she was glad the trembling was rage, and not fear. Suppose he had fallen dead of a heart attack or something, after all her efforts to protect him that day!

"What's that you say? Speak up, I will not tolerate this mumbling. Stop fussing me, Roberta, and take back this pebble or whatever it is. Now, young man——"

Great-Uncle Felix stopped. "Where's the boy gone?"

For Roberta the shape against the hedge remained, and the voice in her head spoke.

"Remember. Do not let go of me, or you destroy my chance of death."

"Most extraordinary. He's completely vanished——" Great-Uncle Felix turned abruptly on her, and she had to put up her hands to fend off the collision. "Did you see where he went? Must have gone like the wind. Put the fear of God into him, anyway." He seemed satisfied, and took hold of her arm in an almost jovial way to steer her towards the house, but she knew, without looking, that they were alone. Her head was dizzy with what had happened, with the fear of that other world, with the strain of listening, and she let herself be propelled along the gravel without resistance.

"Astonishing nerve the boy has, coming here almost directly after I had thrown them both out. You have to admire him, you know. It takes courage to defy a Featherstone. They could have told you that at a few battles in our history. But darting away like that, childish, very childish. Of course, it's easy enough to disappear in this garden, used to do it myself when I didn't want to be found when I was a boy—used to fancy I had a friend, you know, an only child often does that. Mind that briar, must tell Moss to prune it before it blinds someone—we, my friend and I— used to have many an adventure together, though I must have been lonelier than I realised, now I think back; the friend I made up, very clearly, mind you, I could see him as distinctly as that young Pack a minute ago, he was a melancholy kind of fellow,

117

I would get quite low when I had fancied anything for too long. Ah, here we are. You had better get your hot milk and wheat-germ from Mrs. Pigeon while I bolt the door."

So Great-Uncle Felix had known him too, and thought he'd made him up. It was, suddenly, horribly sad, perhaps because it put him into a different perspective, appearing to a lonely child some sixty years ago—yet who knew how long he had been around this garden? Perhaps he had been at its making, and that would have been four hundred years ago, according to Mrs. Pigeon. Had he hoped for some help from Great-Uncle Felix once, before he grew up? The garden might have seen many children in those centuries, but none had been able to do anything for him. Now she had a chance, and she wasn't going to let him down.

# CHAPTER

## 15

Eleven-thirty found her sitting on the edge of her four-poster, still wondering what to do. She hadn't dared lie down in case she fell asleep, even sitting up she had caught herself reclining peacefully against one of the columns of the bed not as though it were wood, carved so that it stuck into her, but more as if it were the softest of pillows. After that, she sat well in the middle so that if she reclined she would have to topple over. With any luck that might wake her up.

But falling asleep was a minor worry compared to the rest of what lay before her. He hadn't said anything about midnight this time, but that was always supposed to be the magic time, when things happened. It had to be the Knowe, too, and she would have to get there again. That meant going through the clipped yews once more.

This second time of going to the Knowe was worse, because now in a sort of way she knew what to expect, and the fear of it was cold in her stomach. He had said they would be angry at anyone trying to take him away, and the less she thought about that the better. She was his only chance, and she had to do it.

Suddenly resolute, she got up, hardly even feeling sleepy any more, and put on her blazer again. It might be cold going through the garden now, and a pocket was useful for carrying the elfstone. She touched it fleetingly, just to make sure it was there, and wondered if Great-Uncle Felix had one too, once, when he had played in the gardens as a child with his imaginary companion, or whether different rules had applied then and it hadn't been necessary. But boys often kept stones they liked in their pockets, and he might never have connected the appearance of his friend with holding the stone. Thinking of that made her want to cry, though, he had waited so long for help; and she shook the hair out of her eyes, glanced at her watch—it was twenty to twelve—and opened the door of her room slowly and carefully.

The corridor outside was silent. Moonlight spilled through a window at the end, silvering the air all round, but first she had to tread through the shadows to the stairs leading down to the black hall. As before, each tread regretted the step she was taking, and it seemed impossible no one would hear. Any minute now the cry "Roberta!" would ring in her ears, and that precious chance would be lost, perhaps for ever.

No cry came, the door responded obediently to the elfstone and she stepped out into the cooler air of the garden. When she came to them the yews held less menace than before, or perhaps it was just that everything paled beside what she was going to do.

It took longer than she had expected, getting through the field to the Knowe; the surface of the ground was uneven and, in spite of the moon, it was hard to see where she was putting her feet. She didn't, after all, want to twist her ankle again and not make it to the Knowe in time.

As she reached the Knowe she heard midnight striking faintly on the wind, and felt in her pocket for the elfstone. This time she actually saw the door open in the side of the Knowe, a slit of light outlined it and grew as the door opened before her. Light, scent, music, all poured out as before but now she felt she entered of her own will—not drawn in dazed—taking the step with intent, however terrified.

She crossed the threshold and paused, feeling rather than hearing the door close behind her. There was no dancing this evening, they were waiting for her, seated in rows like some court of justice, a glittering circle in the shadows. She began to walk towards the throne—no point now in thinking it wasn't or, indeed, arguing with herself about the identity of the one who sat on it. Her face was in shadow but the scent from her clothes, as she leant forward, was again the smell of primroses and violets, fresh, sweet and wild.

"Human wit has triumphed!" The voice had laughter in it, and Bertie felt a surge of resentment stiffening her resolve. So human beings were pathetic, a world of Laurels and Hardys in comparison with the cool elegance all around her, but that didn't mean they could be played with like toys, punished, stolen.

"We sent for you so that you might know our gratitude. Ever have we given gifts to those who please us——"

Try as she would, remembering suddenly how her thoughts could be read, Bertie could not prevent the image of withered leaves presenting itself.

"—and mocked those who did not. Our gold remains gold, though it may not pass for such in your world. You would be wise to ask for something in that world of yours and not from ours."

Was that a warning, a threat? But the voice was almost coaxing.

"What will you have? We have treasure of other kind than gold."

"What kind?" Bertie thought stubbornly of the leaves, they were useful as a kind of thought-protection.

"You have seen our powers of inflicting pain. Do you not wish to know if we can heal also?"

The leaves Bertie had concentrated on to guard her mind seemed to blow away, and she could not prevent the picture that came of Daddy, ill after the crash, as she had seen him in the hospital bed, strapped up and bandaged, the one good eye that smiled at her purpled with a bruise all round. And was She hinting at healing marriages too?

"You must trust our skill." The voice was soft in her head, like a breeze breathing through the grass, immensely soothing. "We can do what you wish."

Bertie shook her head, she wasn't sure why, as though to get rid of something, but already she had forgotten what. The movement of her head, however, was echoed somewhere, as her eyes moved with her head, they saw, for a brief instant, outside the radius of light coming from that throne. Among the golden faces

121

ranged round, like those of angels in some illuminated picture come alive, was one pale one, earth-pale, with dark and hopeless eyes.

She found herself running forward, brushing past the silken skirts that hissed aside from her like angry cats, and seizing his arm. It was a human arm, hard and steady under the satin sleeve.

"I choose him!"

All around her was a sound like thunder as they rose. Cutting through that was the voice, shrill as ice.

"Keep him if you can!"

There was sudden darkness like a blow. She clung to that arm but to her infinite terror it shrank in her grip. Somewhere in her memory were his words, "Do not slack your grip, however I may change", and she put all her strength into that hold on something that was dissolving in her grasp, that was no longer a human arm. Pictures now rose in the darkness faster than she could ward them off, of deformities, of dwarves, of mutilations, like a sickening filmreel of a mixture of hospitals and battle-fields. Her fingers were curling away when she remembered, suddenly, the smile on the face of a thalidomide child, with only knobs for arms, racing about on a go-kart. She tightened her hand.

The thing under it was too round now, it had a slippery, power-ful feel, growing in size, swelling under her hand. It was dry, too, warm, even scaly. In the second in which her brain relayed the information, she knew what it meant. It was not possible to hold a snake in that grip, in which it had already begun to writhe.

The scaly muscle rippled, crawled under her clutching fingers, whipped to and fro, growing all the time. She had terrified visions of a python, its monstrous coils oozing nearer her in the dark. Any minute they would grip her round her waist, her chest, her neck, across her mouth—or was it a cobra that would strike at her suddenly? Would she feel the dreadful whispering of its tongue flickering over her, exploring before it struck?

It was the memory of his eyes that made her hold on. They had no hope; she would show him that there was hope. The snake was in her mind, but she was really hanging on to him.

The snake had gone almost as suddenly as it had come, but it left her feeling numb, both in her mind and hands. In the dark she was afraid she had let go of his arm without realising it. Her brain sent the message to her fingers to tighten their grip and, as far as she knew, her fingers obeyed—except that there was nothing to hold. Nothing like an arm, that was. She held it, though, wondering. It came to her that it was like an arm, as an X-ray is like a photograph of someone. She was holding the bones of an arm, the arm of a skeleton.

She could hear her own scream deafening her, slitting the darkness, but to her own flinching astonishment she held on, even while she waited for the other arm to grip her, for something beyond all nightmare to happen. She shut her eyes, unable to do anything now but whimper and gasp, and hang on to that unthinkable arm.

It was the wind blowing about her face that made her open her eyes. What she shrank from seeing was not there. He was there, standing gravely with his arm in her grasp, without speaking, and behind him the Knowe in the rosy light of dawn. They were outside, the door had shut, he was won into her world.

# CHAPTER
## 16

He was looking at the sun now, and she followed his eyes. She hadn't seen many dawns, and this one was special, as though she had never quite thought of the sun coming up over the rim of the world before. But it isn't, she thought confusedly, we're coming up over it; or round it, at least. Yet she had, as she looked with him, a solemn sense of it being their star they looked at, the sun of the solar system that lit them both as human beings.

"I have to thank you for this." His face was no longer earth-pale, but coloured by the dawn as he turned to her. She felt suddenly humbled by his courtesy.

"You saved me first. I mean, you warned me about Them. I might easily have eaten what they offered, or drunk the wine." The thought of what might have happened was dizzying, even while she put it from her.

"Could I see you suffer as I had suffered?"

She thought of the weary centuries, and looked down. The breeze spoke in the hair of the Knowe and she shivered.

"Shouldn't we go? Is it safe?"

"They do not break their word. I am given forth from their company for ever, thank God." He glanced back at the sun, as though gratitude were due there.

"What are you going to do now?" It had suddenly come to her that whereas she had a house and a bed to go to, a great-uncle, and a family at home, he had nothing. If he had had a family they must have died somewhere back in the Middle Ages. If she took him back with her, how could she explain him to Great-Uncle Felix? "This is a hippy friend of mine, can he come to stay?" He looked hippy enough, with his long hair, fringed tunic and boots, but what kind of a scene would that provoke, after the tiff with Gawain? Great-Uncle Felix wasn't exactly keen on her friends at the moment, let alone anyone she might bring back at dawn.

"I have something more to ask of you yet."

She was disgusted with herself that she felt immediately tired, immediately frightened. Wasn't what she had just gone through enough for anyone to ask?

"This is the last thing I shall burden you with." He said it gently and without reproach, and she instantly put out a hand towards him in apology, and was surprised to see him draw back from her.

"I am in this world now. You must not touch me yet. Take me to the church." She had to think about that. What church did he mean? She hadn't been to a church, but of course she hadn't been here for Sunday yet. It was difficult to realise, having been in two worlds as she had been, in two different times, that she hadn't even been a week at Longbarrow. She didn't even know what day it was. Still, if he wanted to get to church, she would take him.

"I'll take you. Only I don't know where it is."

His finger pointed, and following its direction she saw, a little way beyond the house and partly hidden by trees, the glint of a spire in the first rays of the sun. A doubt grew in her. She wanted to ask him how he knew where the church was, whether he came from some place in the neighbourhood, but she was stopped by the idea of his family being dead, he might not want to talk about it at all. Anyway, when she remembered how he was accustomed to wander about the grounds, it wouldn't be very surprising if he did get to know where the church was after just about four hundred years in which to notice the spire she had happened to miss in four days.

Walking away from the Knowe was just as dream-like as walking to it had been; now, in the early morning light turning from rose to gold, dizzy and light-headed from the weariness of two nights spent practically without sleep, she felt they were like two ghosts in a sleeping world. Only the rough going in the meadow kept her awake and, in fact, she found it possible to sleep in the second it took to put her foot down, and one part of her mind was interested in this. She woke again when she put her hand on the white-painted gate that led from field to yew-garden, slap into the puddle of cold dew on the top of it. She had decided, in so far as she was able to decide anything, that it would be quickest to go through the garden, skirting the house—it was easier walking than in the fields, for one thing—and go out down the drive, turn left at the road and follow it to the clump of trees that had seemed to shelter the spire. It would have to be visible from the road. Anyway—she woke again as she tripped on a tilted flagstone on the terrace and saved herself with a hand on the house-wall—he knew the way.

The next time she seemed to come properly awake again was in front of the church itself. She dimly recollected a lych-gate, that funny sort of gate with a hat on like a well, that you get in front of some old churchyards; and walking up some gravel that crunched like brittle toffee; and then the church stood before her. She woke up because it had a presence, just as the Knowe had. You couldn't ignore it, it breathed out something serene. They both looked up at its height, at the lichened stone, the bell-tower, the spire against the deepening blue of the sky. She wondered fleetingly how old it was, whether it had been built when he had gone into the Knowe.

"You must take me in."

Take him in? She wondered why he couldn't just go by himself instead of asking her, and he turned, as she hesitated, a face of deep sadness.

"We have both been in an unholy place, but you were free of it, and I was bound in my flesh and blood."

"You mean—the food you took?" It was uncomfortable thinking of one's digestive system forming a link with an invisible world, but it made sense all the same.

He nodded, and gestured, with that sad courtesy, at the weather-stained oak door. "You must be my conduct into a hallowed place."

126

She put her hand on the great iron ring-handle and turned it. The door was locked.

"I expect it won't be open until the Vicar comes and unlocks it for service—that is, if it's Sunday. Or the Verger, or whoever lets the cleaners in. I shouldn't think that'll be for ages yet, the sun's only just coming up."

He clasped his hands at his chest and she was shocked to see him distressed. His calm, his resignation, his hopelessness she had got used to; it seemed that now, suddenly, some hope he had allowed himself at last had disturbed him deeply.

"Must I wait yet longer? Can I never rest?"

Bertie thought of something and put her hand in her pocket. The elfstone was still there. Hadn't he said it was an Opener? It had opened the doors in the house as well as the Knowe itself. Not that she wanted to think about that now, it was just that she couldn't bear to see that look of pain, rather than sadness on his face. She had a feeling, though, as she brought the elfstone out of her pocket, that it had not lost its danger, and she heard him call out, in that moment when her eyes took that now familiar jolt and the focus of everything changed—"Lay hold of the ring!"

Without pausing to think, in a second of blind obedience that luckily recognised what "the ring" was, she grasped the cold iron of the great handle. In that second, the earth ceased to turn beneath her feet as though to cast her into another world, the man at her side swam back and steadied from wherever he was disappearing to, and the great lock ground its teeth and yawned the door open.

"Cast it from you!" (She knew well what he meant, and still clinging to the door-handle that had dragged her with it in that uncanny moment, she flung the elfstone into the bushes that clustered untidily round the church. She knew then, though she didn't know why, that it was safe to let go of the handle.

"Had I known you possessed that still, I would never have urged you to use it; all you won was nearly lost."

"They couldn't have taken you back, could they? I mean, they promised."

"Put yourself in their power, as you did, and they might be

tempted. Their world is not to be entered lightly, as we have both found; and not by using their means."

Bertie found her knees weak as though she had just got up from a bout of flu. She had to sit down. Now the door was open, she could see, through the gloom of the porch, the lines of seats in the church, and she went to one thankfully. He came through the porch and stood for a moment on the threshold, looking down, and then, slowly, gravely, entered the church. In spite of her exhaustion, she realised that something significant had happened.

It was a bit difficult, in a way, to understand. Bertie hadn't been that number of times in church herself—to a service, that is. Her parents went occasionally, to weddings and christenings, of course, but not often on ordinary Sundays. She had visited quite a few, sight-seeing, but that wasn't the same, though she had been in some churches where just being in them made you feel different, as though their shape, or something in the air as well as the arrangement of stones all round, touched a place in you. You didn't want to talk, or even look at the interesting bits, just stand there and get the message, whatever it was.

He had passed her, and was standing, looking down the church, without moving. She got up and joined him, but as she stood beside him she knew she couldn't really join him. If there were a message in that place, he was getting it, and she still didn't know what it was. He began to walk down the aisle towards the altar, the soft leather of his boots making no sound on the stone so that she was awkwardly conscious of her noisy shoes following.

He stopped by a carving set into the wall. It was very old and worn, a representation of a man kneeling with his hands pressed together in prayer. Underneath there was something chiselled out in what looked like Latin. He stretched a hand towards it as though he were going to stroke the words.

"So they remembered me."

"Is that supposed to be you? But you're not dead. I mean, I thought they didn't put up things to people in churches if they weren't buried there."

He smiled slightly, and she thought, that's the first time I've seen him do that. "You cannot bury where there is no body."

She looked more closely at the kneeling figure, and touched it. It felt cold and rough under her fingers. "I suppose it was a case of 'Missing, presumed dead' when you didn't come back. From wherever they thought you had gone, that is. Did they, could they, have had any idea?"

"In the days when I lived" (it was eerie hearing him say that; after all, he was living now, wasn't he?) "men understood more about the Knowe of Featherstone than some may now. They may have hoped, whatever they suspected, to give me what safety they might by placing my likeness in a holy place. And am I not here, in the end?"

He spoke more strongly, so that his voice, which she now remembered she had first heard in her head, rang round the church, in a challenge, in triumph. "I have been in bondage, I have been weary beyond man's telling, but the time for rest has come, God be thanked."

He turned to her and extended a hand, as though to take hers in farewell. Instinctively, she took it, and saw on his face for a fleeting moment as he turned his eyes towards the altar behind her, a smile to which the one she had already seen was only a pale shadow. She had read of people's faces being transformed by joy, but she realised that she had never known what it meant until that second.

It was only a second for, in the next, he was gone. In a flash of time, his shape hung in the air but the light from the window streamed through it urgently, as though dispersing it. Gold dust whirled, there was a touch as though of feathers in the palm of her hand and a voice again in her head which did not speak but without words blessed her.

# CHAPTER

## 17

It was cold. Mother must have forgotten to turn the radiator on. It must be late, too, or Mother wouldn't be shaking her like this. She must try to wake up, or she would be late for school. It was difficult to try, though, as she seemed to be numb with the cold and very far away, but she did make an enormous effort and opened her eyes.

It was not Mother's face that was so close to hers. Mother didn't have dark hair and she certainly didn't wear those owl-like glasses. She really did know who it was, yet it was too much bother remembering.

"Are you all right? Did you faint or something? What's wrong? What on earth are you doing in here anyway?"

There were luckily far too many questions for her to have to answer any of them. She closed her eyes again.

"Oh glory, hang on a bit, I'll go and get . . ."

Bertie, still with her eyes closed, heard feet running away, and the hollow echo of them made her remember that she was in a church. She was a little surprised, but prepared to accept the fact. Her memory also informed her that the name of the person who had bent over her was Clothilde and that for some reason or other she didn't particularly care for her. She could hear someone, possibly Clothilde, shouting outside the church but she couldn't hear what.

Now there was a double set of feet at the run, and this time coming towards her. A hand, a cool thin hand, the touch of which she instinctively liked, took hers and she let it be taken.

"Bertie. Have you hurt yourself, Bertie? Try to tell us."

There were two faces looking at her now, and she read the expressions with mild interest. They were anxious. The lenses of Clothilde's glasses were tinted a rather beautiful pale rose. Rose-coloured spectacles. They gave you a cheerful view on life.

"I'm all right. I think I fell asleep."

She began to struggle to sit up, but it was painful as her legs and arms seemed to have stayed asleep after the rest of her, and she was glad of Gawain's help. He didn't try to pull her up or make her stand or anything silly like that, the way people usually did when you had fallen over or weren't well. He simply crouched beside her and propped her, partly against him and partly against the wall behind.

"How did you get into the church anyway? It's supposed to be locked. I came along here at this unearthly hour to do a brass-rubbing before the service started, and the vicar gave me the key. When I found the door open I expected to find someone had made off with the altar candlesticks and not you kipping in a heap in the chancel."

Just like Clothilde, Bertie thought, to know it was the chancel she was in. Gawain hadn't asked her any questions, he simply went on holding her hand and, as she felt herself growing less numb, it was as though it was from him the warmth was gradually spreading.

"It gave me quite a turn, actually. Thought I'd done a sort of Dr. Who timeslip and stumbled on someone looking for sanctuary."

That was a word that did make sense. Sanctuary was when you got away from people and God protected you, whatever you had done and whatever had happened to you. That, and the word 'timeslip', brought it back, and she shut her eyes again, tightly, in refuge against the dust he had become. It seemed perfectly natural, too, to put her head down on Gawain's shoulder and start crying. She was always crying these days. It seemed to be just as difficult to stop as sneezing was when you had a cold. She didn't even mind particularly crying in front of Clothilde,

131

which showed you, she thought, that she really had got into this crying thing, as normally the only person she would let see her cry was Mother, and not often at that. She was saying things, too, mixed with the crying, which she hadn't intended either.

"He's gone . . . gone into nothing . . . it was horrible."

Horrible wasn't the right word for it, it wasn't fair to call it horrible, but her sense of shock had to be expressed somehow.

"Who's gone? Has somebody tried to hurt you?"

She dimly realised they were thinking of tramps, attacks, really horrible things but a world away from what she was remembering, the human dust that had dissolved in her hand.

"No . . . I'm all right, nobody touched me." She had touched him, that was it, he had stopped her touching him until he was ready to go. He had known what would happen, but he couldn't have thought what it would be like to her.

"Did someone come into the church? Was someone after the candlesticks after all?"

"It wasn't anything like that. We came together. He wanted to get to the church because he wanted to die properly, at last." She couldn't go on for a bit after that, and put her face back in Gawain's shoulder, which smelt quite like home. She could hear Clothilde, over her head, asking plaintively if she were out of her mind, and where was the corpse. Gawain's voice, when he answered, vibrated in his chest against her ear.

"Leave her alone, Clot. Some funny things have happened to her."

"Such as?"

"She can tell you if she wants to."

"I think she's ill. She looks ghastly. Probably her uncle's driven her round the twist. Do you think he's the one who's dropped dead?"

"Well, you could go out and scout around in case he has. If he's dropped in here he's done it behind something."

"O.K. I'll look in the graveyard."

The idea of Clothilde peering about among the tombstones for dead bodies was suddenly hilarious to Bertie, she began to laugh, weakly because now she was feeling exhausted, and Gawain must have thought she was crying again because he actually stroked her hair.

"Do you really call her Clot?"

He seemed a little surprised at the question. "She calls me Gaga, so it's fair do's. There's an unwritten thing about not in public but with your emergency I forgot."

Clot and Gaga, thought Bertie dreamily. How human they had turned out to be, even Clothilde, compared to the supercilious beings from another planet they had seemed at first. Perhaps it was only seeing those who were not human that made one realise companionship of one's own kind. Thinking like that made her feel better; she had known all along she had to help him, whether or not she wanted to. She took her mind away from the motes of dust dancing in the sun's rays, to listen to Gawain.

"What exactly were you doing here? Was it anything to do with the man you saw—the messenger?"

It was so easy explaining things to Gawain, he was already half-way there.

"How did you guess?"

"I had a sort of idea things might end up here. Clothilde isn't the only one who's done her folk stuff homework. Anyone in the land you went into who comes to his senses wants out, but usually can't make it without help. You were the only one who could help, weren't you?"

Bertie nodded, remembering the thunder of their silken skirts as They rose, the darkness in which he had changed under her clinging hands into shapes and things she could not have borne to see.

"I thought he'd be able to come back here again. I thought I was doing it for that."

"Do you mean the church, or this world?"

"I mean this world, life, you know."

"Did he want to come to the church, or did you think of it?"

"Oh no, he led me here. He had said something about not letting go of him because—it would ruin his chances of death, I think he said." She hid her face again, and heard Gawain's voice in his chest say,

"Don't talk about it if you'd rather not. I take it that he got

133

what he wanted, whatever it was, so you must have helped him."

That was exactly the way she had been trying to think of it, but it sounded convincing when he said it. She freed herself abruptly, ignoring the threads of hair that caught on his jersey, and looked at him. He was rather unnervingly close, but, for once, he looked perfectly serious.

"Gawain. Do you believe in heaven and things like that?"

"You've chosen a jolly awkward place to ask me in. Anyway, if you mean do I think he's banging away at a harp in his nightie, no, but if you mean out of this world and at peace after suffering, yes."

She thought to herself that *centuries* of suffering certainly did qualify as suffering. Gawain's definition satisfied her and she felt, for the first time for ages, the beginnings of cheerfulness. She saw the reflection of her own growing smile in his face, and for a moment they were both happy just to look at one another.

The moment was short-lived, however, for footsteps hurried down the aisle.

"Get up this instant, sir! Roberta, what do you mean by publicly embracing this vagabond here? And as for you, I told you expressly to stay away from me and mine!"

"You can hardly prevent me, Mr. Featherstone," Gawain was courteously helping her to her feet, "from coming to church. It's quite usual on Sundays."

Great-Uncle Felix made a noise like bacon sizzling in a frying-pan, but he had clearly decided to tackle his more vulnerable opponent first.

"I would like to know, Roberta, why you have stolen away from the house to make an assignation with this creature here?"

In spite of his fury, he was trying to keep his voice down because of where they were; Bertie found this oddly touching. Clothilde was hovering behind him, making exaggerated gestures of horror and apology at them, and Bertie found herself actually liking her. Poor old Clot, running out to look for the corpse of Great-Uncle Felix and finding it only too lively.

"An explanation, Roberta, that is what I require. I come out here for a little healthful exercise before breakfast and to observe the architectural glories of this church, and I discover this female," he glanced sharply round and caught Clothilde in the middle of a particularly gruesome grimace, "conducting herself like a madwoman peering about among the gravestones. Having had but the slenderest trust in the sanity of her family for some time, I am not surprised when she behaves as though she has seen a ghost when I address her. As I gather from her antics that something is happening in the church that she doesn't want me to interrupt, I naturally come here straight away. I am waiting for an explanation."

Bertie stared at him wordlessly. If that was what he was waiting for, they'd better resign themselves to being there a long time. With any luck, there'd be a service there at some point, and they'd have to stop standing and staring at each other.

As if pat on the cue of her thought, came brisker, more professional footsteps, and they were hailed by a voice that did not have scruples about raising itself under an accustomed roof.

"Ah, Mr. Featherstone! I didn't expect to see you here so early, and these young friends of yours." (Bertie thought Great-Uncle Felix's moustache would burst its moorings at this description.) "We don't usually have such a good turn-out for the early service. I'm quite relieved to find you here. When I saw the door was open, I was beginning to think we'd had a break-in, you know, our candlesticks are Charles II and very good silver, we are always a little afraid for them in these terrible times." He was busy shaking hands with them while he was talking and Bertie had a sudden feeling that he was really rather shy and wanted to hold them at bay with words. For a moment she pictured Great-Uncle Felix as a wild boar, tusks drooling, stamping to get at them, and found herself saying, as the Vicar took her hand,

"I'm Roberta Morton, Mr. Featherstone's great-niece, and I'm staying with him. This is Clothilde and Gawain Pack——"

"Ah, yes, the children of our famous archaeologist. Delighted to meet you all, come to worship together like this." He was shooing them, little by little, up to the top pew, Bertie realised, and glanced at Great-Uncle Felix. He seemed to be speechless.

"We've all heard about the coming dig at the Knowe, Mr. Featherstone." (If he explodes, Bertie thought, they'll have instant frescoes in this church.) "I can't help thinking it's an excellent idea, and I do hope Mr. Pack will think of employing a little local labour, the Cubs would be so pleased to help, I know, even if it was only putting in the markers——"

"There will be *no* dig." Great-Uncle Felix spoke with such intensity that the Vicar glanced at him nervously, like a man who has been strolling on the lip of a volcano without realising it. "Nobody is going to meddle with the Knowe, let alone——" He stopped, moustache twitching, and Bertie thought he had suddenly seen he couldn't start on his flood of abuse about Mr. Pack in front of the Vicar. It must be horribly frustrating for him, especially with Gawain politely inclined towards him as though anxious not to miss a word.

"Dear, dear, no dig? I must have got all my information wrong, but then by now I should really know better than to believe all I hear in the village. You'll be popular with some people, Mr. Featherstone, for I can't deny there's a lot of unfortunate superstition about the Knowe, but I always say the best way you can counteract superstition is with religion itself. Faith in the right things will win in the end, you know."

He had been rummaging about with his back to them under the top shelf of the front pew, and now he turned, his round face triumphant, and pressed prayer-books into their hands.

"I'm so glad to see you all friends still, in spite of Mr. Pack's natural disappointment, it's a truly Christian spirit that brings you all here together like this, and I'm only sorry Mr. Pack himself couldn't be with you, but another time, no doubt. Now I won't keep you waiting any longer, luckily I'm already robed, can't keep my things in the vestry now, alas, with the damp the way it is, my wife doesn't think it's healthy." He had turned again, this time from the step up to the altar, and his voice was different; they were still people but they were also, now, a congregation.

"Dearly beloved brethren, the Scripture moveth us in sundry places . . ."

Bertie went quickly, and as quietly as she could, into the pew. After a second, Great-Uncle Felix followed her, and she was conscious, beyond him, of Gawain and Clothilde meekly taking their places. Bertie wondered if they had ever attended any service other than their own christenings, the Packs were the sort of people who were probably brought up to believe religion *was* superstition, anyway. Out of the corner of her eye, however, she could see them competently finding their way through the prayer-book. Great-Uncle Felix she wasn't sure about, the Vicar hadn't seemed too surprised at finding him in church, so perhaps he did do the conventional thing on Sundays from time to time, but one thing she was convinced of, he was finding this service a strain. Well, religion wasn't meant to be easy, you wouldn't have to be told about it, and reminded of it in church if it were. If Great-Uncle Felix was really trying to forgive the trespasses committed against him, it might be the biggest thing that had ever happened to him.

"Ye that do truly and earnestly repent you of your sins, and are in love and charity with your neighbours, and intend to lead a new life . . ."

Could people hear things like that and go on being beastly to their neighbours? People did, though, all the same. Would Great-Uncle Felix ever make it up with the Packs, or would she and Gawain not be able to see each other again? Somehow, that wasn't believable. Faith seemed to belong in a church, and, at the moment, she had faith in a number of things. She had tried to help someone, and it had worked; people had helped her, too. Daddy was going to be helped, she was somehow sure of that. They would be a family again. There were curious things in the world, and out of it, that couldn't be explained—even scientists had come around to admitting that. The Knowe wasn't a place she intended to go near again, even when Great-Uncle Felix had built his Folly on it. It was funny they hadn't minded the Folly, perhaps they saw it as a tribute, a kind of decoration. All the same, she hoped nobody would fall asleep in it.

". . . for this is my blood of the New Testament, which is shed for you and for many for the remission of sins: do this, as oft as ye shall drink it, in remembrance of me."

Great-Uncle Felix got up stiffly, and made his way past Gawain and Clothilde to go up to take Communion. As he passed Gawain, who rose to give him room to go by, he put out a hand without looking at him, and pressed him down again into his seat, patting the shoulder as he went.

Bertie put her face back into her hands and wondered what the Vicar would do if she started bawling out loud, for sheer happiness, in the middle of the service.